Prairie Folks

Hamlin Garland

Alpha Editions

This edition published in 2024

ISBN 9789361470073

Design and Setting By

Alpha Editions

www.alphaedis.com

Email - info@alphaedis.com

Contents

Prairie Folks.

Pioneers.

They rise to mastery of wind and snow;
    They go like soldiers grimly into strife,
To colonize the plain; they plow and sow,
    And fertilize the sod with their own life
As did the Indian and the buffalo.

Settlers.

Above them soars a dazzling sky,
    In winter blue and clear as steel,
In summer like an Arctic sea
    Wherein vast icebergs drift and reel
And melt like sudden sorcery.

Beneath them plains stretch far and fair,
    Rich with sunlight and with rain;
Vast harvests ripen with their care
    And fill with overplus of grain
Their square, great bins.

Yet still they strive! I see them rise
    At dawn-light, going forth to toil:
The same salt sweat has filled my eyes,
    My feet have trod the self-same soil
Behind the snarling plow.

Part I.

UNCLE ETHAN'S SPECULATION IN PATENT MEDICINES.

A certain guileless trust in human kind
Too often leads them into nets
Spread by some wandering trader,
Smooth, and deft, and sure.

UNCLE ETHAN RIPLEY.

UNCLE ETHAN had a theory that a man's character could be told by the way he sat in a wagon seat.

"A mean man sets right plumb in the *middle* o' the seat, as much as to say, 'Walk, gol darn yeh, who cares?' But a man that sets in one corner o' the seat, much as to say, 'Jump in—cheaper t' ride 'n to walk,' you can jest tie to."

Uncle Ripley was prejudiced in favor of the stranger, therefore, before he came opposite the potato patch, where the old man was "bugging his vines." The stranger drove a jaded-looking pair of calico ponies, hitched to a clattering democrat wagon, and he sat on the extreme end of the seat, with the lines in his right hand, while his left rested on his thigh, with his little finger gracefully crooked and his elbows akimbo. He wore a blue shirt, with gay-colored armlets just above the elbows, and his vest hung unbuttoned down his lank ribs. It was plain he was well pleased with himself.

As he pulled up and threw one leg over the end of the seat, Uncle Ethan observed that the left spring was much more worn than the other, which proved that it was not accidental, but that it was the driver's habit to sit on that end of the seat.

"Good afternoon," said the stranger, pleasantly.

"Good afternoon, sir."

"Bugs purty plenty?"

"Plenty enough, I gol! I don't see where they all come fum."

"Early Rose?" inquired the man, as if referring to the bugs.

"No; Peachblows an' Carter Reds. My Early Rose is over near the house. The old woman wants 'em near. See the darned things!" he pursued, rapping savagely on the edge of the pan to rattle the bugs back.

"How do yeh kill 'em—scald 'em?"

"Mostly. Sometimes I"——

"Good piece of oats," yawned the stranger, listlessly.

"That's barley."

"So 'tis. Didn't notice."

Uncle Ethan was wondering what the man was. He had some pots of black paint in the wagon, and two or three square boxes.

"What do yeh think o' Cleveland's chances for a second term?" continued the man, as if they had been talking politics all the while.

Uncle Ripley scratched his head. "Waal—I dunno—bein' a Republican—I think "——

"That's so—it's a purty scaly outlook. I don't believe in second terms myself," the man hastened to say.

"Is that your new barn acrost there?" pointing with his whip.

"Yes, sir, it is," replied the old man, proudly. After years of planning and hard work he had managed to erect a little wooden barn, costing possibly three hundred dollars. It was plain to be seen he took a childish pride in the fact of its newness.

The stranger mused. "A lovely place for a sign," he said, as his eyes wandered across its shining yellow broadside.

Uncle Ethan stared, unmindful of the bugs crawling over the edge of his pan. His interest in the pots of paint deepened.

"Couldn't think o' lettin' me paint a sign on that barn?" the stranger continued, putting his locked hands around one knee, and gazing away across the pig-pen at the building.

"What kind of a sign? Gol darn your skins!" Uncle Ethan pounded the pan with his paddle and scraped two or three crawling abominations off his leathery wrist.

It was a beautiful day, and the man in the wagon seemed unusually loath to attend to business. The tired ponies slept in the shade of the lombardies. The plain was draped in a warm mist, and shadowed by vast, vaguely defined masses of clouds—a lazy June day.

"Dodd's Family Bitters," said the man, waking out of his abstraction with a start, and resuming his working manner. "The best bitter in the market." He alluded to it in the singular. "Like to look at it? No trouble to show goods, as the fellah says," he went on hastily, seeing Uncle Ethan's hesitation.

He produced a large bottle of triangular shape, like a bottle for pickled onions. It had a red seal on top, and a strenuous caution in red letters on the neck, "None genuine unless 'Dodd's Family Bitters' is blown in the bottom."

"Here's what it cures," pursued the agent, pointing at the side, where, in an inverted pyramid, the names of several hundred diseases were arranged, running from "gout" to "pulmonary complaints," etc.

"I gol! she cuts a wide swath, don't she?" exclaimed Uncle Ethan, profoundly impressed with the list.

"They ain't no better bitter in the world," said the agent, with a conclusive inflection.

"What's its speshy-*a*ty? Most of 'em have some speshy-*a*ty."

"Well—summer complaints—an'—an'—spring an' fall troubles—tones ye up, sort of."

Uncle Ethan's forgotten pan was empty of his gathered bugs. He was deeply interested in this man. There was something he liked about him.

"What does it sell fur?" he asked, after a pause.

"Same price as them cheap medicines—dollar a bottle—big bottles, too. Want one?"

"Wal, mother ain't to home, an' I don't know as she'd like this kind. We ain't been sick f'r years. Still, they's no tellin'," he added, seeing the answer to his objection in the agent's eyes. "Times is purty close, too, with us, y' see; we've jest built that stable "——

"Say, I'll tell yeh what I'll do," said the stranger, waking up and speaking in a warmly generous tone. "I'll give you ten bottles of the bitter if you'll let me paint a sign on that barn. It won't hurt the barn a bit, and if you want 'o, you can paint it out a year from date. Come, what d' ye say?"

"I guess I hadn't better."

The agent thought that Uncle Ethan was after more pay, but in reality he was thinking of what his little old wife would say.

"It simply puts a family bitter in your home that may save you fifty dollars this comin' fall. You can't tell."

Just what the man said after that Uncle Ethan didn't follow. His voice had a confidential purring sound as he stretched across the wagon-seat and talked on, eyes half shut. He straightened up at last, and concluded in the tone of one who has carried his point:

"So! If you didn't want to use the whole twenty-five bottles y'rself, why! sell it to your neighbors. You can get twenty dollars out of it easy, and still have five bottles of the best family bitter that ever went into a bottle."

It was the thought of this opportunity to get a buffalo-skin coat that consoled Uncle Ethan as he saw the hideous black letters appearing under the agent's lazy brush.

It was the hot side of the barn, and painting was no light work. The agent was forced to mop his forehead with his sleeve.

"Say, hain't got a cooky or anything, and a cup o' milk handy?" he said at the end of the first enormous word, which ran the whole length of the barn.

Uncle Ethan got him the milk and cooky, which he ate with an exaggeratedly dainty action of his fingers, seated meanwhile on the staging which Uncle Ripley had helped him to build. This lunch infused new energy into him, and in a short time "DODD'S FAMILY BITTERS, Best in the Market," disfigured the sweet-smelling pine boards.

Ethan was eating his self-obtained supper of bread and milk when his wife came home.

"Who's been a-paintin' on that barn?" she demanded, her bead-like eyes flashing, her withered little face set in an ominous frown. "Ethan Ripley, what you been doin'?"

"Nawthin'," he replied, feebly.

"Who painted that sign on there?"

"A man come along an' he wanted to paint that on there, and I let 'im; and it's my barn, anyway. I guess I can do what I'm a min' to with it," he ended, defiantly; but his eyes wavered.

Mrs. Ripley ignored the defiance. "What under the sun p'sessed you to do such a thing as that, Ethan Ripley? I declare I don't see! You git fooler an' fooler ev'ry day you live, I *do* believe."

Uncle Ethan attempted a defense.

"Well, he paid me twenty-five dollars f'r it, anyway."

"Did 'e?" She was visibly affected by this news.

"Well, anyhow, it amounts to that; he give me twenty-five bottles"——

Mrs. Ripley sank back in her chair. "Well, I swan to Bungay! Ethan Ripley—wal, you beat all I *ever* see!" she added in despair of expression."I thought you had *some* sense left, but you hain't, not one blessed scimpton. Where *is* the stuff?"

"Down cellar, an' you needn't take on no airs, ol' woman. I've known you to buy things you didn't need time an' time 'n' agin, tins and things, an' I guess you wish you had back that ten dollars you paid for that illustrated Bible."

"Go 'long an' bring that stuff up here. I never see such a man in my life. It's a wonder he didn't do it fr two bottles." She glared out at the sign, which faced directly upon the kitchen window.

Uncle Ethan tugged the two cases up and set them down on the floor of the kitchen. Mrs. Ripley opened a bottle and smelled of it like a cautious cat.

"Ugh! Merciful sakes, what stuff! It ain't fit fr a hog to take. What'd you think you was goin' to do with it?" she asked in poignant disgust.

"I expected to take it—if I was sick. Whaddy ye s'pose?" He defiantly stood his ground, towering above her like a leaning tower.

"The hull cartload of it?"

"No. I'm goin' to sell part of it an' git me an overcoat"——

"Sell it!" she shouted. "Nobuddy'll buy that sick'nin' stuff but an old numbskull like you. Take that slop out o' the house this minute! Take it right down to the sink-hole an' smash every bottle on the stones."

Uncle Ethan and the cases of medicine disappeared, and the old woman addressed her concluding remarks to little Tewksbury, her grandson, who stood timidly on one leg in the doorway, like an intruding pullet.

"Everything around this place 'ud go to rack an' ruin if I didn't keep a watch on that soft-pated old dummy. I thought that lightenin'-rod man had give him a lesson he'd remember, but no, he must go an' make a reg'lar"———

She subsided in a tumult of banging pans, which helped her out in the matter of expression and reduced her to a grim sort of quiet. Uncle Ethan went about the house like a convict on shipboard. Once she caught him looking out of the window.

"I should *think* you'd feel proud o' that."

Uncle Ethan had never been sick a day in his life. He was bent and bruised with never-ending toil, but he had nothing especial the matter with him.

He did not smash the medicine, as Mrs. Ripley commanded, because he had determined to sell it. The next Sunday morning, after his chores were done, he put on his best coat of faded diagonal, and was brushing his hair into a ridge across the center of his high, narrow head, when Mrs. Ripley came in from feeding the calves.

"Where you goin' now?"

"None o' your business," he replied. "It's darn funny if I can't stir without you wantin' to know all about it. Where's Tewky?"

"Feedin' the chickens. You ain't goin' to take him off this mornin' now! I don't care where you go."

"Who's a-goin' to take him off? I ain't said nothin' about takin' him off."

"Wall, take y'rself off, an' if y' ain't here f'r dinner, I ain't goin' to get no supper."

Ripley took a water-pail and put four bottles of "the bitter" into it, and trudged away up the road with it in a pleasant glow of hope. All nature seemed to declare the day a time of rest, and invited men to disassociate ideas of toil from the rustling green wheat, shining grass, and tossing blooms. Something of the sweetness and buoyancy of all nature permeated the old man's work-calloused body, and he whistled little snatches of the dance tunes he played on his fiddle.

But he found neighbor Johnson to be supplied with another variety of bitter, which was all he needed for the present. He qualified his refusal to buy with a cordial invitation to go out and see his shotes, in which he took infinite pride. But Uncle Ripley said: "I guess I'll haf t' be goin'; I want 'o git up to Jennings' before dinner."

He couldn't help feeling a little depressed when he found Jennings away. The next house along the pleasant lane was inhabited by a "new-comer." He was sitting on the horse-trough, holding a horse's halter, while his hired man dashed cold water upon the galled spot on the animal's shoulder.

After some preliminary talk Ripley presented his medicine.

"Hell, no! What do I want of such stuff? When they's anything the matter with me, I take a lunkin' ol' swig of popple-bark and bourbon. That fixes me."

Uncle Ethan moved off up the lane. He hardly felt like whistling now. At the next house he set his pail down in the weeds beside the fence, and went in without it. Doudney came to the door in his bare feet, buttoning his suspenders over a clean boiled shirt. He was dressing to go out.

"Hello, Ripley. I was just goin' down your way. Jest wait a minute an' I'll be out."

When he came out fully dressed, Uncle Ethan grappled him.

"Say, what d' you think o' paytent med"——

"Some of 'em are boss. But y' want 'o know what y're gitt'n'."

"What d' ye think o' Dodd's"—— -

"Best in the market."

Uncle Ethan straightened up and his face lighted. Doudney went on:

"Yes, sir; best bitter that ever went into a bottle. I know, I've tried it. I don't go much on patent medicines, but when I get a good"——

"Don't want 'o buy a bottle?"

Doudney turned and faced him.

"Buy! No. I've got nineteen bottles I want 'o *sell*." Ripley glanced up at Doudney's new granary and there read "Dodd's Family Bitters." He was stricken dumb. Doudney saw it all and roared.

"Wal, that's a good one! We two tryin' to sell each other bitters. Ho—ho—ho—har, whoop! wal, this is rich! How many bottles did you git?"

"None o' your business," said Uncle Ethan, as he turned and made off, while Doudney screamed with merriment.

On his way home Uncle Ethan grew ashamed of his burden. Doudney had canvassed the whole neighborhood, and he practically gave up the struggle. Everybody he met seemed determined to find out what he had been doing, and at last he began lying about it.

"Hello, Uncle Ripley, what y' got there in that pail?"

"Goose eggs f'r settin'."

He disposed of one bottle to old Gus Peterson. Gus never paid his debts, and he would only promise fifty cents "on tick" for the bottle, and yet so desperate was Ripley that this *quasi* sale cheered him up not a little.

As he came down the road, tired, dusty and hungry, he climbed over the fence in order to avoid seeing that sign on the barn, and slunk into the house without looking back.

He couldn't have felt meaner about it if he had allowed a Democratic poster to be pasted there.

The evening passed in grim silence, and in sleep he saw that sign wriggling across the side of the barn like boa-constrictors hung on rails. He tried to paint them out, but every time he tried it the man seemed to come back with a sheriff, and savagely warned him to let it stay till the year was up. In some mysterious way the agent seemed to know every time he brought out the paint-pot, and he was no longer the pleasant-voiced individual who drove the calico ponies.

As he stepped out into the yard next morning, that abominable, sickening, scrawling advertisement was the first thing that claimed his glance—it blotted out the beauty of the morning.

Mrs. Ripley came to the window, buttoning her dress at the throat, a whisp of her hair sticking assertively from the little knob at the back of her head.

"Lovely, ain't it! An' *I*'ve got to see it all day long. I can't look out the winder but that thing's right in my face." It seemed to make her savage. She hadn't been in such a temper since her visit to New York. "I hope you feel satisfied with it."

Ripley walked off to the barn. His pride in its clean, sweet newness was gone. He slyly tried the paint to see if it couldn't be scraped off, but it was dried in thoroughly. Whereas before he had taken delight in having his neighbors turn and look at the building, now he kept out of sight whenever he saw a team coming. He hoed corn away in the back of the field, when he should have been bugging potatoes by the roadside.

Mrs. Ripley was in a frightful mood about it, but she held herself in check for several days. At last she burst forth:

"Ethan Ripley, I can't stand that thing any longer, and I ain't goin' to, that's all! You've got to go and paint that thing out, or I will. I'm just about crazy with it."

"But, mother, I promised "——

"I don't care *what* you promised, it's got to be painted out. I've got the nightmare now, seein' it. I'm goin' to send f'r a pail o' red paint, and I'm goin' to paint that out if it takes the last breath I've got to do it."

"I'll tend to it, mother, if you won't hurry me"——

"I can't stand it another day. It makes me boil every time I look out the winder."

Uncle Ethan hitched up his team and drove gloomily off to town, where he tried to find the agent. He lived in some other part of the county, however, and so the old man gave up and bought a pot of red paint, not daring to go back to his desperate wife without it.

"Goin' to paint y'r new barn?" inquired the merchant, with friendly interest.

Uncle Ethan turned with guilty sharpness; but the merchant's face was grave and kindly.

"Yes, I thought I'd touch it up a little—don't cost much."

"It pays—always," the merchant said emphatically.

"Will it—stick jest as well put on evenings?" inquired Uncle Ethan, hesitatingly.

"Yes—won't make any difference. Why? Ain't goin' to have"——

"Waal,—I kind o' thought I'd do it odd times night an' mornin'—kind o' odd times"——

He seemed oddly confused about it, and the merchant looked after him anxiously as he drove away.

After supper that night he went out to the barn, and Mrs. Ripley heard him sawing and hammering. Then the noise ceased, and he came in and sat down in his usual place.

"What y' ben makin'?" she inquired. Tewksbury had gone to bed. She sat darning a stocking.

"I jest thought I'd git the stagin' ready f'r paintin'," he said, evasively.

"Waal! I'll be glad when it's covered up." When she got ready for bed, he was still seated in his chair, and after she had dozed off two or three times she began to wonder why he didn't come. When the clock struck ten, and she realized that he had not stirred, she began to get impatient. "Come, are y' goin' to sit there all night?" There was no reply. She rose up in bed and looked about the room. The broad moon flooded it with light, so that she could see he was not asleep in his chair, as she had supposed. There was something ominous in his disappearance.

"Ethan! Ethan Ripley, where are yeh?" There was no reply to her sharp call. She rose and distractedly looked about among the furniture, as if he might somehow be a cat and be hiding in a corner somewhere. Then she went upstairs where the boy slept, her hard little heels making a curious *tunking* noise on the bare boards. The moon fell across the sleeping boy like a robe of silver. He was alone.

She began to be alarmed. Her eyes widened in fear. All sorts of vague horrors sprang unbidden into her brain. She still had the mist of sleep in her brain.

She hurried down the stairs and out into the fragrant night. The katydids were singing in infinite peace under the solemn splendor of the moon. The cattle sniffed and sighed, jangling their bells now and then, and the chickens in the coops stirred uneasily as if overheated. The old woman stood there in her bare feet and long nightgown, horror-stricken. The ghastly story of a man who had hung himself in his barn because his wife deserted him came into her mind and stayed there with frightful persistency. Her throat filled chokingly.

She felt a wild rush of loneliness. She had a sudden realization of how dear that gaunt old figure was, with its grizzled face and ready smile. Her breath came quick and quicker, and she was at the point of bursting into a wild cry to Tewksbury, when she heard a strange noise. It came from the barn, a creaking noise. She looked that way, and saw in the shadowed side a deeper shadow moving to and fro. A revulsion to astonishment and anger took place in her.

"Land o' Bungay! If he ain't paintin' that barn, like a perfect old idiot, in the night."

Uncle Ethan, working desperately, did not hear her feet pattering down the path, and was startled by her shrill voice.

"Well, Ethan Ripley, whaddy y' think you're doin' now?"

He made two or three slapping passes with the brush, and then snapped, "I'm a-paintin' this barn—whaddy ye s'pose? If ye had eyes y' wouldn't ask."

"Well, you come right straight to bed. What d'you mean by actin' so?"

"You go back into the house an' let me be. I know what I'm a-doin'. You've pestered me about this sign jest about enough." He dabbed his brush to and fro as he spoke. His gaunt figure towered above her in shadow. His slapping brush had a vicious sound.

Neither spoke for some time. At length she said more gently, "Ain't you comin' in?"

"No—not till I get a-ready. You go 'long an' tend to y'r own business. Don't stan' there an' ketch cold."

She moved off slowly toward the house. His voice subdued her. Working alone out there had rendered him savage; he was not to be pushed any farther. She knew by the tone of his voice that he must not be assaulted. She slipped on her shoes and a shawl, and came back where he was working, and took a seat on a saw-horse.

"I'm a-goin' to set right here till you come in, Ethan Ripley," she said, in a firm voice, but gentler than usual.

"Waal, you'll set a good while," was his ungracious reply. But each felt a furtive tenderness for the other. He worked on in silence. The boards creaked heavily as he walked to and fro, and the slapping sound of the paint-brush sounded loud in the sweet harmony of the night. The majestic moon swung slowly round the corner of the barn, and fell upon the old man's grizzled head and bent shoulders. The horses inside could be heard stamping the mosquitoes away, and chewing their hay in pleasant chorus.

The little figure seated on the saw-horse drew the shawl closer about her thin shoulders. Her eyes were in shadow, and her hands were wrapped in her shawl. At last she spoke in a curious tone.

"Well, I don't know as you *was* so very much to blame. I *didn't* want that Bible myself—I held out I did, but I didn't."

Ethan worked on until the full meaning of this unprecedented surrender penetrated his head, and then he threw down his brush.

"Waal, I guess I'll let 'er go at that. I've covered up the most of it, anyhow. Guess we'd better go in."

30

31

PART II.

THE TEST OF ELDER PILL
THE COUNTRY PREACHER.

The lonely center of their social life,
The low, square school-house, stands
Upon the wind-swept plain,
Hacked by thoughtless boyish hands,
And gray, and worn, and warped with strife
Of sleet and autumn rain.

ELDER PILL, PREACHER.

I.

OLD MAN BACON was pinching forked barbs on a wire fence one rainy day in July, when his neighbor Jennings came along the road on his way to town. Jennings never went to town except when it rained too hard to work outdoors, his neighbors said; and of old man Bacon it was said he *never* rested *nights* nor Sundays.

Jennings pulled up. "Good morning, neighbor Bacon."

"Mornin'," rumbled the old man without looking up.

"Taking it easy, as usual, I see. Think it's going to clear up?"

"May, an' may not. Don't make much differunce t' me," growled Bacon, discouragingly.

"Heard about the plan for a church?"

"Naw."

"Well, we're goin' to hire Elder Pill from Douglass to come over and preach every Sunday afternoon at the school-house, an' we want help t' pay him—the laborer is worthy of his hire."

"Sometimes he is an' then agin he ain't. Y' needn't look t' me f'r a dollar. I ain't got no intrust in y'r church."

"Oh, yes, you have—besides, y'r wife "——

"She ain't got no more time 'n I have t' go t' church. We're obleeged to do 'bout all we c'n stand t' pay our debts, let alone tryun' to support a preacher." And the old man shut the pinchers up on a barb with a vicious grip.

Easy-going Mr. Jennings laughed in his silent way. "I guess you'll help when the time comes," he said, and, clucking to his team, drove off.

"I guess I won't," muttered the grizzled old giant as he went on with his work. Bacon was what is called land-poor in the West, that is, he had more land than money; still he was able to give if he felt disposed. It remains to say that he was *not* disposed, being a sceptic and a scoffer. It angered him to have Jennings predict so confidently that he would help.

The sun was striking redly through a rift in the clouds, about three o'clock in the afternoon, when he saw a man coming up the lane, walking on the grass at the side of the road, and whistling merrily. The old man looked at him from under his huge eyebrows with some curiosity. As he drew near, the pedestrian ceased to whistle, and, just as the farmer expected him to pass, he stopped and said, in a free and easy style:

"How de do? Give me a chaw t'baccer. I'm Pill, the new minister. I take fine-cut when I can get it," he said, as Bacon put his hand into his pocket. "Much obliged. How goes it?"

"Tollable, tollable," said the astounded farmer, looking hard at Pill as he flung a handful of tobacco into his mouth.

"Yes, I'm the new minister sent around here to keep you fellows in the traces and out of hell-fire. Have y' fled from the wrath?" he asked, in a perfunctory way.

"You are, eh?" said Bacon, referring back to his profession.

"I am just! How do you like that style of barb fence? Ain't the twisted wire better?"

"I s'pose they be, but they cost more."

"Yes, costs more to go to heaven than to hell. You'll think so after I board with you a week. Narrow the road that leads to light, and broad the way that leads—how's your soul anyway, brother?"

"Soul's all right. I find more trouble to keep m' body go'n'."

"Give us your hand; so do I. All the same we must prepare for the next world. We're gettin' old; lay not up your treasures where moth and rust corrupt and thieves break through and steal."

Bacon was thoroughly interested in the preacher, and was studying him carefully. He was tall, straight, and superbly proportioned; broad-shouldered, wide-lunged, and thewed like a Greek racer. His rather small steel-blue eyes twinkled, and his shrewd face and small head, set well back, completed a remarkable figure. He wore his reddish beard in the usual way of Western clergymen, with mustache chopped close.

Bacon spoke slowly:

"You look like a good, husky man to pitch in the barnyard; you've too much muscle f'r preachun'."

"Come and hear me next Sunday, and if you say so then, I'll quit," replied Mr. Pill, quietly. "I give ye my word for it. I believe in preachers havin' a little of the flesh and the devil; they can sympathize better with the rest of ye." The sarcasm was lost on Bacon, who continued to look at him. Suddenly he said, as if with an involuntary determination:

"Where ye go'n' to stay t'night?"

"I don' know; do you?" was the quick reply.

"I reckon ye can hang out with me, 'f ye feel like ut. We ain't very purty, ol' woman an' me, but we eat. You go along down the road and tell 'er I sent yeh. Y'll find an' ol' dusty Bible round some'rs—I s'pose ye spend y'r spare time read'n about Joshua an' Dan'l"——

"I spend more time reading men. Well, I'm off! I'm hungrier 'n a gray wolf in a bear-trap." And off he went as he came. But he did not whistle; he chewed.

Bacon felt as if he had made too much of a concession, and had a strong inclination to shout after him, and retract his invitation; but he did not, only worked on, with an occasional bear-like grin. There was something captivating in this fellow's free and easy way.

When he came up to the house an hour or two later, in singular good humor for him, he found the Elder in the creamery, with "the old woman" and Marietta. Marietta was not more won by him than was Jane Bacon, he was so genial and put on so few religious frills.

Mrs. Bacon never put on frills of any kind. She was a most frightful toiler, only excelled (if excelled at all) by her husband. She was still muscular in her age and shapelessness. Unlovely at her best, when about her work in her faded calico gown and flat shoes, hair wisped into a slovenly knot, she was depressing. But she was a good woman, of sterling integrity, and ambitious for her girl.

Marietta was as attractive as her mother was depressing. She was very young at this time and had the physical perfection—at least as regards body—that her parents must have had in youth. She was above the average height of woman, with strong swell of bosom and glorious, erect carriageof head. Her features were coarse, but regular and pleasing, and her manner boyish.

Elder Pill was on the best of terms with them as he watched the milk being skimmed out of the "submerged cans" ready for the "caaves and hawgs," as Mrs. Bacon called them.

"Dad told you t' come here 'nd stay t' supper, did he? What's come over him?" said the girl, with a sort of audacious humor.

"Dad has an awful grutch agin preachers," said Mrs. Bacon, as she wiped her hands on her apron. "I declare, I don't see how"——

"*Some* preachers, not *all* preachers," laughed Pill, in his mellow nasal. "There are preachers, and then again preachers. I'm one o' the t'other kind."

"I sh'd think y' was," laughed the girl.

"Now, Merry Etty, you run right t' the pig-pen with that milk, whilst I go in an' set the tea on."

Mr. Pill seized the can of milk, saying, with a twang: "Show me the way that I may walk therein," and, accompanied by the laughing girl, made rapid way to the pig-pen just as the old man set up a ferocious shout to call the hired hand out of the cornfield.

"How'd y' come to send *him* here?" asked Mrs. Bacon, nodding toward Pill.

"Damfino! I kind o' liked him—no nonsense about him," answered Bacon, going into temporary eclipse behind his hands as he washed his face at the cistern.

At the supper table Pill was "easy as an old shoe," ate with his knife, talked on fatting hogs, suggested a few points on raising clover, told of pioneer experiences in Michigan, and soon won them—hired man and all—to a most favorable opinion of himself. But he did not trench on religious matters at all.

The hired man in his shirt-sleeves, and smelling frightfully of tobacco and sweat (as did Bacon), sat with open month, at times forgetting to eat, in his absorbing interest in the minister's yarns.

"Yes, I've got a family, too much of a family, in fact—that is, I think so sometimes when I'm pinched. Our Western people are so indigent—in plain terms, poor—they *can't* do any better than they do. But we pull through—we pull through! John, you look like a stout fellow, but I'll bet a hat I can *down* you three out of five."

"I bet you can't," grinned the hired man. It was the climax of all, that bet.

"I'll take y' in hand an' flop y' both," roared Bacon from his lion-like throat, his eyes glistening with rare good-nature from the shadow of his gray brows. But he admired the minister's broad shoulders at the same time. If this fellow panned out as he promised, he was a rare specimen.

After supper the Elder played a masterly game of croquet with Marietta, beating her with ease; then he wandered out to the barn and talked horses with the hired man, and finished by stripping off his coat and putting on one of Mrs. Bacon's aprons to help milk the cows.

But at breakfast the next morning, when the family were about pitching into their food as usual without ceremony, "*Wait!*" said the visitor, in an imperious tone and with lifted hand. "Let us look to the Lord for His blessing."

They waited till the grace was said, but it threw a depressing atmosphere over the meal; evidently they considered the trouble begun. At the end of the meal the minister asked:

"Have you a Bible in the house?"

"I reckon there's one in the house somewhere. Merry, go 'n see 'f y' can't raise one," said Mrs. Bacon, indifferently.

"Have you any objection to family devotion?" asked Pill, as the book was placed in his hands by the girl.

"No; have all you want," said Bacon, as he rose from the table and passed out the door.

"I guess I'll see the thing through," said the hand. "It ain't just square to leave the women folks to bear the brunt of it."

It was shortly after breakfast that the Elder concluded he'd walk up to Brother Jennings' and see about church matters.

"I shall expect you, Brother Bacon, to be at the service at 2:30."

"All right, go ahead expectun'," responded Bacon, with an inscrutable sidewise glance.

"You promised, you remember?"

"The—devil—I did!" the old man snarled.

The Elder looked back with a smile, and went off whistling in the warm, bright morning.

II.

THE school-house down on the creek was known as "Hell's Corners" all through the county, because of the frequent rows that took place therein at "corkuses" and the like, and also because of the number of teachers that had been "ousted" by the boys. In fact, it was one of those places still to be found occasionally in the West, far from railroads and schools, where the primitive ignorance and ferocity of men still prowl, like the panthers which are also found sometimes in the deeps of the Iowa timber lands.

The most of this ignorance and ferocity, however, was centered in the family of Dixons, a dark-skinned, unsavory group of Missourians. It consisted of old man Dixon and wife, and six sons, all man-grown, great, gaunt, sinewy fellows, with no education, but superstitious as savages. If anything went wrong in 'Hell's Corners' everybody knew that the Dixons were "on the rampage again." The school-teachers were warned against the Dixons, and the preachers were besought to convert the Dixons.

In fact, John Jennings, as he drove Pill to the school-house next day, said:

"If you can convert the Dixon boys, Elder, I'll give you the best horse in my barn."

"I work not for such hire," said Mr. Pill, with a look of deep solemnity on his face, belied, indeed, by a twinkle in his small, keen eye—a twinkle which made Milton Jennings laugh candidly.

There was considerable curiosity, expressed by a murmur of lips and voices, as the minister's tall figure entered the door and stood for a moment in a study of the scene before him. It was a characteristically Western scene. The women were rigidly on one side of the school-room, the men as rigidly on the other; the front seats were occupied by squirming boys and girls in their Sunday splendor.

On the back, to the right, were the young men, in their best vests, with paper collars and butterfly neckties, with their coats unbuttoned, their hair plastered down in a fascinating wave on their brown foreheads. Not a few were in their shirt-sleeves. The older men sat immediately betweenthe youths and boys, talking in hoarse whispers across the aisles about the state of the crops and the county ticket, while the women in much the same way conversed about children and raising onions and strawberries. It was their main recreation, this Sunday meeting.

"Brethren!" rang out the imperious voice of the minister, "let us pray."

The audience thoroughly enjoyed the Elder's prayer. He was certainly gifted in that direction, and his petition grew genuinely eloquent as his desires embraced the "ends of the earth and the utterm'st parts of the seas thereof." But in the midst of it a clatter was heard, and five or six strapping fellows filed in with loud thumpings of their brogans.

Shortly after they had settled themselves with elaborate impudence on the back seat, the singing began. Just as they were singing the last verse, every individual voice wavered and all but died out in astonishment to see William Bacon come in—an unheard-of thing! And with a clean shirt, too! Bacon, to tell the truth, was feeling as much out of place as a cat in a bath-tub, and looked uncomfortable, even shamefaced, as he sidled in, his shapeless hat gripped nervously in both hands; coatless and collarless, his shirt open at his massive throat. The girls tittered, of course, and the boys hammered each other's ribs, moved by the unusual sight. Milton Jennings, sitting beside Marietta, said:

"Well! may I jump straight up and never come down!"

And Shep Watson said: "May I never see the back o' my neck!" Which pleased Marietta so much that she grew purple with efforts to conceal her laughter; she always enjoyed a joke on her father.

But all things have an end, and at last the room became quiet as Mr. Pill began to read the Scripture, wondering a little at the commotion. He suspected that those dark-skinned, grinning fellows on the back seat were the Dixon boys, and knew they were bent on fun. The physique of the minister being carefully studied, the boys began whispering among themselves, and at last, just as the sermon opened, they began to push the line of young men on the long seat over toward the girls' side, squeezing Milton against Marietta. This pleasantry encouraged one of them to whack his neighbor over the head with his soft hat, causing great laughter and disturbance. The preacher stopped. His cool, penetrating voice sounded strangely unclerical as he said:

"There are some fellows here to-day to have fun with me. If they don't keep quiet, they'll have more fun than they can hold." At this point a green crab-apple bounded up the aisle. "I'm not to be bulldozed."

He pulled off his coat and laid it on the table before him, and, amid a wondering silence, took off his cuffs and collar, saying:

"I can preach the word of the Lord just as well without my coat, and I can throw rowdies out the door a little better in my shirt-sleeves."

Had the Dixon boys been a little shrewder as readers of human character, or if they had known why old William Bacon was there, they would have kept quiet; but it was not long before they began to push again, and at last one of them gave a squeak, and a tussle took place. The preacher was in the midst of a sentence:

"An evil deed, brethren, is like unto a grain of mustard seed. It is small, but it grows steadily, absorbing its like from the earth and air, sending out roots and branches, till at last"———

There was a scuffle and a snicker. Mr. Pill paused, and gazed intently at Tom Dixon, who was the most impudent and strongest of the gang; then he moved slowly down on the astonished young savage. As he came his eyes seemed to expand like those of an eagle in battle, steady, remorseless, unwavering, at the same time that his brows shut down over them—a glance that hushed every breath. The awed and astounded ruffians sat as if paralyzed by the unuttered yet terribly ferocious determination of the preacher's eyes. His right hand was raised, the other was clenched at his waist. There was a sort of solemnity in his approach, like a tiger creeping upon a foe.

At last, after what seemed minutes to the silent, motionless congregation, his raised hand came down on the shoulder of the leader with the exact, resistless precision of the tiger's paw, and the ruffian was snatched from his seat to the floor sprawling. Before he could rise, the steel-like grip of the roused preacher sent him half way to the door, and then out into the dirt of the road.

Turning, Pill came back down the aisle; as he came the half-risen congregation made way for him, curiously. When he came within reach of Dick, the fellow struck savagely out at the preacher, only to have his blow avoided by a lithe, lightning-swift movement of the body above the hips (a trained boxer's trick), and to find himself also lying bruised and dazed on the floor.

By this time the rest of the brothers had recovered from their stupor, and, with wild curses, leaped over the benches toward the fearless Pill.

But now a new voice was heard in the sudden uproar—a new but familiar voice. It was the raucous snarl of William Bacon, known far and wide as a terrible antagonist, a man who had never been whipped. He was like a wild beast excited to primitive savagery by the smell of blood.

"*Stand back*, you hell-hounds!" he said, leaping between them and the preacher. "You know me. Lay another hand on that man an', by the livun' God, you answer t' me. Back thear!"

Some of the men cheered, most stood irresolute. The women crowded together, the children began to scream with terror, while through it all Pill was dragging his last assailant toward the door.

Bacon made his way down to where the Dixons had halted, undecided what to do. If the preacher had the air and action of the tiger, Bacon looked the grizzly bear—his eyebrows working up and down, his hands clenched into frightful bludgeons, his breath rushing through his hairy nostrils.

"Git out o' hyare," he growled. "You've run things here jest about long enough. Git out!"

His hands were now on the necks of two of the boys, and he was hustling them toward the door.

"If you want 'o whip the preacher, meet him in the public road—one at a time; he'll take care o' himself. Out with ye," he ended, kicking them out. "Show your faces here agin, an' I'll break ye in two."

The non-combative farmers now began to see the humor of the whole transaction and began to laugh; but they were cut short by the calm voice of the preacher at his desk:

"But a *good* deed, brethren, is like unto a grain of wheat planted in good earth, that bringeth forth fruit in due season an hundred fold."

III.

MR. PILL, with all his seeming levity, was a powerful hand at revivals, as was developed at the "protracted" meetings held at the Corners during December. Indeed, such was the pitiless intensity of his zeal that a gloom was cast over the whole township; the ordinary festivities stopped or did not begin at all.

The lyceum, which usually began by the first week in December, was put entirely out of the question, as were the spelling-schools and "exhibitions." The boys, it is true, still drove the girls to meeting in the usual manner; but they all wore a furtive, uneasy air, and their laughter was not quite genuine at its best, and died away altogether when they came near the school-house, and they hardly recovered from the effects of the preaching till a mile or two had been spun behind the shining runners. It took all the magic of the jingle of the bells and the musical creak of the polished steel on the snow to win them back to laughter.

As for Elder Pill, he was as a man transformed. He grew more intense each night, and strode back forth behind his desk and pounded the Bible like an assassin. No more games with the boys, no more poking the girls under the chin! When he asked for a chew of tobacco now it was with an air which said: "I ask it as sustenance that will give me strength for the Lord's service," as if the demands of the flesh had weakened the spirit.

Old man Bacon overtook Milton Jennings early one Monday morning, as Milton was marching down toward the Seminary at Rock River. It was intensely cold and still, so cold and still that the ring of the cold steel of the heavy sleigh, the snort of the horses, and the old man's voice came with astonishing distinctness to the ears of the hurrying youth, and it seemed a very long time before the old man came up.

"Climb on!" he yelled, out of his frosty beard. He was seated on the "hind bob" of a wood-sleigh, on a couple of blankets. Milton clambered on, knowing well he'd freeze to death there.

"Reckon I heerd you prowlun' around the front door with my girl last night," Bacon said at length. "The way you both 'tend out t' meetun' ought 'o sanctify yeh; must 'a' stayed to the after-meetun', didn't yeh?"

"Nope. The front part was enough for"——

"Danged if I was any more fooled with a man in m' life. I b'lieve the whole thing is a little scheme on the bretheren t' raise a dollar."

"Why so?"

"Waal, y' see Pill ain't got much out o' the app'intment thus fur, and he ain't likely to, if he don't shake 'em up a leetle. Borrud ten dollars o' me t'other day."

Well, thought Milton, whatever his real motive is, Elder Pill is earning all he gets. Standing for two or three hours in his place night after night, arguing, pleading, but mainly commanding them to be saved.

Milton was describing the scenes of the meeting to Bradley Talcott and Douglas Radbourn the next day, and Radbourn, a young law student said:

"I'd like to see him. He must be a character."

"Let's make up a party and go out," said Milton, eagerly.

"All right; I'll speak to Lily Graham."

Accordingly, that evening a party of students, in a large sleigh, drove out toward the school-house, along the drifted lanes and through the beautiful aisles of the snowy woods. A merry party of young people, who had no sense of sin to weigh them down. Even Radbourn and Lily joined in the songs which they sang to the swift clanging of the bells, until the lights of the school-house burned redly through the frosty air.

Not a few of the older people present felt scandalized by the singing and by the dancing of the "town girls," who could not for the life of themtake the thing seriously. The room was so little, and hot, and smoky, and the men looked so queer in their rough coats and hair every which-way.

But they took their seats demurely on the back seat, and joined in the opening songs, and listened to the halting prayers of the brethren and the sonorous prayers of the Elder, with commendable gravity. Miss Graham was a devout Congregationalist, and hushed the others into gravity when their eyes began to dance dangerously.

However, as Mr. Pill warmed to his work, the girls grew sober enough. He awed them, and frightened them with the savagery of his voice and manner. His small gray eyes were like daggers unsheathed, and his small, round head took on a cat-like ferocity, as he strode to and fro, hurling out his warnings and commands in a hoarse howl that terrified the sinner, and drew 'amens' of admiration from the saints.

"Atavism; he has gone back to the era of the medicine man," Radbourn murmured.

As the speaker went on, foam came upon his thin lips; his lifted hand had prophecy and threatening in it. His eyes reflected flames; his voice had now the tone of the implacable, vindictive judge. He gloated on the pictures that his words called up. By the power of his imagination the walls widened, the floor was no longer felt, the crowded room grew still as death, every eye fixed on the speaker's face.

"I tell you, you must repent or die. I can see the great judgment angel now!" he said, stopping suddenly and pointing above the stove-pipe. "I can see him as he stands weighing your souls as a man 'ud weigh wheat and chaff. Wheat goes into the Father's garner; chaff is blown to hell's devouring flame! I can see him *now*! He seizes a poor, damned, struggling soul by the *neck*, he holds him over the flaming forge of *hell* till his bones melt like wax; he shrivels like thread in a flame of a candle; he is nothing but a charred husk, and the angel flings him back into *outer darkness*; life was not in him."

It was this astonishing figure, powerfully acted, that scared poor Tom Dixon into crying out for mercy. The effect on the rest was awful. To see so great a sinner fall terror-stricken seemed like a providential stroke of confirmatory evidence, and nearly a dozen other young people fell crying. Whereat the old people burst out into amens with unspeakable fervor. But the preacher, the wild light still in his eyes, tore up and down, crying above the tumult:

"The Lord is come with *power*! His hand is visible *here*. Shout *aloud* and spare *not*. Fall before him as *dust* to his feet! Hypocrites, vipers, scoffers! the *lash* o' the *Lord* is on ye!"

In the intense pause which followed as he waited with expectant, uplifted face—a pause so deep even the sobbing sinners held their breath—a dry, drawling, utterly matter-of-fact voice broke the tense hush.

"S-a-y, Pill, ain't you a bearun' down on the boys a *leetle too* hard?"

The preacher's extended arm fell as if life had gone out of it. His face flushed and paled; the people laughed hysterically, some of them the tears of terror still on their cheeks; but Radbourn said, "Bravo, Bacon!"

Pill recovered himself.

"Not hard enough for *you*, neighbor Bacon."

Bacon rose, retaining the same dry, prosaic tone:

"I ain't bitin' that kind of a hook, an' I ain't goin' to be *yanked* into heaven when I c'n *slide* into hell. Waal! I must be goin'; I've got a new-milk's cow that needs tendin' to."

The effect of all this was indescribable. From being at the very mouth of the furnace, quivering with fear and captive to morbid imaginings, Bacon's dry intonation had brought them all back to earth again. They saw a little of the absurdity of the whole situation.

Pill was beaten for the first time in his life. He had been struck below the belt by a good-natured giant. The best he could do, as Bacon shuffled calmly out, was to stammer: "Will some one please sing?" And while they sang, he stood in deep thought. Just as the last verse was quivering into silence, the full, deep tones of Radbourn's voice rose above the bustle of feet and clatter of seats:

"And all *that* he preaches in the name of Him who came bringing peace and good-will to men."

Radbourn's tone had in it reproach and a noble suggestion. The people looked at him curiously. The deacons nodded their heads together in counsel, and when they turned to the desk Pill was gone!

"Gee whittaker! That was tough," said Milton to Radbourn; "knocked the wind out o' him like a cannon-ball. What'll he do now?

"He can't do anything but acknowledge his foolishness."

"You no business t' come here an' 'sturb the Lord's meetin'," cried old Daddy Brown to Radbourn. "You're a sinner and a scoffer."

"I thought Bacon was the disturbing ele"——

"You're just as bad!"

"He's all *right*," said William Councill. "I've got sick, m'self, of bein' *scared* into religion. I never was so fooled in a man in my life. If I'd tell you what Pill said to me the other day, when we was in Robie's store, you'd fall in a fit. An' to hear him talkin' here t'night, is enough to make a horse laugh."

"You're all in league with the devil," said the old man wildly; and so the battle raged on.

Milton and Radbourn escaped from it, and got out into the clear, cold, untainted night.

"The heat of the furnace don't reach as far as the horses," Radbourn moralized, as he aided in unhitching the shivering team. "In the vast, calm spaces of the stars, among the animals, such scenes as we have just seen are impossible." He lifted his hand in a lofty gesture. The light fell on his pale face and dark eyes.

The girls were a little indignant and disposed to take the preacher's part. They thought Bacon had no right to speak out that way, and Miss Graham uttered her protest, as they whirled away on the homeward ride with pleasant jangle of bells.

"But the secret of it all was," said Radbourn in answer, "Pill knew he was acting a part. I don't mean that he meant to deceive, but he got excited, and his audience responded as an audience does to an actor of the first class, and he was for the time in earnest; his imagination *did* see those horrors,— he was swept away by his own words. But when Bacon spoke, his dry tone and homely words brought everybody, preacher and all, back to the earth with a thump! Every body saw that, after weeping and wailing there for an hour, they'd go home, feed the calves, hang up the lantern, put out the cat, wind the clock, and go to bed. In other words, they all came back out of their barbaric *powwow* to their natural modern selves."

This explanation had palpable truth, but Lily had a dim feeling that it had wider application than to the meeting they had just left.

"They'll be music around this clearing to-morrow," said Milton, with a sigh; "wish I was at home this week."

"But what'll become of Mr. Pill?"

"Oh, he'll come out all right," Radbourn assured her, and Milton's clear tenor rang out as he drew Eileen closer to his side:

"O silver moon, O silver moon,
 You set, you set too soon—
 The morrow day is far away,
 The night is but begun."

IV.

THE news, grotesquely exaggerated, flew about the next day, and at night, though it was very cold and windy, the house was jammed to suffocation. On these lonely prairies life is so devoid of anything but work, dramatic entertainments are so few, and appetite so keen, that a temperature of twenty degrees below zero is no bar to a trip of ten miles. The protracted meeting was the only recreation for many of them. The gossip before and after service was a delight not to be lost, and this last sensation was dramatic enough to bring out old men and women who had not dared to go to church in winter for ten years.

Long before seven o'clock, the school-house blazed with light and buzzed with curious speech. Team after team drove up to the door, and as the drivers leaped out to receive the women, they said in low but eager tones to the bystanders:

"Meeting begun yet?"

"Nope!"

"What kind of a time y' havin' over here, any way?"

"A mighty solumn time," somebody would reply to a low laugh.

By seven o'clock every inch of space was occupied; the air was frightful. The kerosene lamps gave off gas and smoke, the huge stove roared itself into an angry red on its jack-oak grubs, and still people crowded in at the door.

Discussion waxed hot as the stove; two or three Universalists boldly attacked everybody who came their way. A tall man stood on a bench in the corner, and, thumping his Bible wildly with his fist, exclaimed, at the top of his voice:

"There is *no* hell at *all!* The Bible says the *wicked* perish *utterly.* They are *consumed* as *ashes* when they die. They *perish* as *dogs!*"

"What kind o' docterin' is that?" asked a short man of Councill.

"I d'know. It's ol' Sam Richards. Calls himself a Christian—Christadelphian 'r some new-fangled name."

At last people began to inquire, "Well, ain't he comin'?"

"Most time f'r the Elder to come, ain't it?"

"Oh, I guess he's preparin' a sermon."

John Jennings pushed anxiously to Daddy Brown.

"Ain't the Elder comin'?"

"I d'know. He didn't stay at my house."

"He didn't?"

"No. Thought he went home with you."

"I ain't see 'im 't all. I'll ask Councill. Brother Councill, seen anything of the Elder?"

"No. Didn't he go home with Bensen?"

"I d'n know. I'll see."

This was enough to start the news that "Pill had skipped."

This the deacons denied, saying "he'd come or send word."

Outside, on the leeward side of the house, the young men who couldn't get in stood restlessly, now dancing a jig, now kicking their huge boots against the underpinning to warm their toes. They talked spasmodically as they swung their arms about their chests, speaking from behind their huge buffalo-coat collars.

The wind roared through the creaking oaks; the horses stirred complainingly, the bells on their backs crying out querulously; the heads of the fortunates inside were shadowed outside on the snow, and the restless young men amused themselves betting on which head was Bensen and which Councill.

At last some one pounded on the desk inside. The suffocating but lively crowd turned with painful adjustment toward the desk, from whence Deacon Benson's high, smooth voice sounded:

"Brethren an' sisters, Elder Pill hain't come—and, as it's about eight o'clock, he probably won't come to-night. After the disturbances last night, it's—a—a—we're all the more determined to—the—a—need of reforming grace is more felt than ever. Let us hope nothing has happened to the Elder. I'll go see to-morrow, and if he is unable to come—I'll see Brother Wheat, of Cresco. After prayer by Brother Jennings, we will adjourn till to-morrow night. Brother Jennings, will you lead us in prayer?" (Some one snickered.) "I hope the disgraceful—a—scenes of last night will not be repeated."

"Where's Pill?" demanded a voice in the back part of the room. "That's what I want to know."

"He's a bad pill," said another, repeating a pun already old.

"I guess so! He borrowed twenty dollars o' me last week," said the first voice.

"He owes me for a pig," shouted a short man, excitedly. "I believe he's skipped to get rid o' his debts."

"So do I. I allus said he was a mighty queer preacher."

"He'd bear watchin' was my idee fust time I ever see him."

"Careful, brethren—*careful*. He may come at any minute."

"I don't care if he does. I'd bone him f'r pay f'r that shote, preacher 'r no preacher," said Bartlett, a little nervously.

- 35 -

High words followed this, and there was prospect of a fight. The pressure of the crowd, however, was so great it was well-nigh impossible for two belligerents to get at each other. The meeting broke up at last, and the people, chilly, soured, and disappointed at the lack of developments, went home saying Pill was *scaly*; no preacher who chawed terbacker was to be trusted; and when it was learned that the horse and buggy he drove he owed Jennings and Bensen for, everybody said, "He's a fraud."

V.

IN the meantime, Andrew Pill was undergoing the most singular and awful mental revolution.

When he leaped blindly into his cutter and gave his horse the rein, he was wild with rage and shame, and a sort of fear. As he sat with bent head, he did not hear the tread of the horse, and did not see the trees glide past. The rabbit leaped away under the shadow of the thick groves of young oaks; the owl, scared from its perch, went fluttering off into the cold, crisp air; but he saw only the contemptuous, quizzical face of old William Bacon—one shaggy eyebrow lifted, a smile showing through his shapeless beard.

He saw the colorless, handsome face of Radbourn, with a look of reproach and a note of suggestion—Radbourn, one of the best thinkers and speakers in Rock River, and the most generally admired young man in Rock County.

When he saw and heard Bacon, his hurt pride flamed up in wrath, but the calm voice of Radbourn, and the look in his stern, accusing eyes, made his head fall in thought. As he rode, things grew clearer. As a matter of fact, his whole system of religious thought was like the side of a shelving sand-bank—in unstable equilibrium—needing only a touch to send it slipping into a shapeless pile at the river's edge. That touch had been given, and he was now in the midst of the motion of his falling faith. He didn't know how much would stand when the sloughing ended.

Andrew Pill had been a variety of things, a farmer, a dry-goods merchant, and a traveling salesman, but in a revival quite like this of his own, he had been converted and his life changed. He now desired to help his fellow-men to a better life, and willingly went out among the farmers, where pay was small. It was not true, therefore, that he had gone into it because there was little work and good pay. He was really an able man, and would have been a success in almost anything he undertook; but his reading and thought, his easy intercourse with men like Bacon and Radbourn, had long since undermined any real faith in the current doctrine of retribution, and to-night, as he rode into the night, he was feeling it all and suffering it all, forced to acknowledge at last what had been long moving.

The horse took the wrong road, and plodded along steadily, carrying him away from his home, but he did not know it for a long time. When at last he looked up and saw the road leading out upon the wide plain between the belts of timber, leading away to Rock River, he gave a sigh of relief. He could not meet his wife then; he must have a chance to think.

Over him, the glittering, infinite sky of winter midnight soared, passionless, yet accusing in its calmness, sweetness and majesty. What was he that he could dogmatize on eternal life and the will of the Being who stood behind that veil? And then would come rushing back that scene inthe school-house, the smell of the steaming garments, the gases from the lamps, the roar of the stove, the sound of his own voice, strident, dominating, so alien to his present mood, he could only shudder at it.

He was worn out with the thinking when he drove into the stable at the Merchants' House and roused up the sleeping hostler, who looked at him suspiciously and demanded pay in advance. This seemed right in his present mood. He was not to be trusted.

When he flung himself face downward on his bed, the turmoil in his brain was still going on. He couldn't hold one thought or feeling long; all seemed slipping like water from his hands.

He had in him great capacity for change, for growth. Circumstances had been against his development thus far, but the time had come when growth seemed to be defeat and failure.

VI.

RADBOURN was thinking about him, two days after, as he sat in his friend Judge Brown's law office, poring over a volume of law. He saw that Bacon's treatment had been heroic; he couldn't get that pitiful confusion of the preacher's face out of his mind. But, after all, Bacon's seizing of just that instant was a stroke of genius.

Some one touched him on the arm.

"Why,—Elder,—Mr. Pill, how de do? Sit down. Draw up a chair."

There was trouble in the preacher's face. "Can I see you, Radbourn, alone?"

"Certainly; come right into this room. No one will disturb us there."

"Now, what can I do for you?" he said, as they sat down.

"I want to talk with you about—about religion," said Pill, with a little timid pause in his voice.

Radbourn looked grave. "I'm afraid you've come to a dangerous man."

"I want you to tell me what you think. I know you're a student. I want to talk about my case," pursued the preacher, with a curious hesitancy. "I want to ask a few questions on things."

"Very well; sail in. I'll do the best I can," said Radbourn.

"I've been thinking a good deal since that night. I've come to the conclusion that I don't believe what I've been preaching. I thought I did, but I didn't. I don't know *what* I believe. Seems as if the land had slid from under my feet. What am I to do?"

"Say so," replied Radbourn, his eyes kindling. "Say so, and get out of it. There's nothing worse than staying where you are. What have you saved from the general land-slide?"

Pill smiled a little. "I don't know."

"Want me to cross-examine you and see, eh? Very well, here goes." He settled back with a smile. "You believe in square dealing between man and man?"

"Certainly."

"You believe in good deeds, candor and steadfastness?"

"I do."

"You believe in justice, equality of opportunity, and in liberty?"

"Certainly I do."

"You believe, in short, that a man should do unto others as he'd have others do unto him; think right and live out his thoughts?"

"All that I steadfastly believe."

"Well, I guess your land-slide was mostly imaginary. The face of the eternal rock is laid bare. You didn't recognize it at first, that's all. One question more. You believe in truth?"

"Certainly."

"Well, truth is only found from the generalizations of facts. Before calling a thing true, study carefully all accessible facts. Make your religion practical. The matter-of-fact tone of Bacon would have had no force if you had been preaching an earnest morality in place of an antiquated terrorism."

"I know it; I know it," sighed Pill, looking down.

"Well, now, go back and tell 'em so. And then, if you can't keep your place preaching what you do believe, get into something else. For the sake of all morality and manhood, don't go on cursing yourself with hypocrisy."

Mr. Pill took a chew of tobacco, rather distractedly, and said:

"I'd like to ask you a few questions."

"No, not now. You think out your present position yourself. Find out just what you have saved from your land-slide."

The elder man rose; he hardly seemed the same man who had dominated his people a few days before. He turned with still greater embarrassment.

"I want to ask a favor. I'm going back to my family. I'm going to say something of what you've said, to my congregation—but—I'm in debt—and the moment they know I'm a backslider, they're going to bear down on me pretty heavy. I'd like to be independent."

"I see. How much do you need?" mused Radbourn.

"I guess two hundred would stave off the worst of them."

"I guess Brown and I can fix that. Come in again to-night. Or no, I'll bring it round to you."

The two men parted with a silent pressure of the hand that meant more than any words.

When Mr. Pill told his wife that he could preach no more, she cried, and gasped, and scolded till she was in danger of losing her breath entirely. "A guinea-hen sort of a woman" Councill called her. "She can talk more an' say less'n any woman I ever see," was Bacon's verdict, after she had been at dinner at his house. She was a perpetual irritant.

Mr. Pill silenced her at last with a note of impatience approaching a threat, and he drove away to the Corners to make his confession without her. It was Saturday night, and Elder Wheat was preaching as he entered the crowded room. A buzz and mumble of surprise stopped the orator for a few moments, and he shook hands with Mr. Pill dubiously, not knowing what to think of it all, but as he was in the midst of a very effective oratorical scene, he went on.

The silent man at his side felt as if he were witnessing a burlesque of himself as he listened to the pitiless and lurid description of torment which Elder Wheat poured forth—the same figures and threats he had used a hundred times. He stirred uneasily in his seat, while the audience paid so littleattention that the perspiring little orator finally called for a hymn, saying:

"Elder Pill has returned from his unexpected absence, and will exhort in his proper place."

When the singing ended, Mr. Pill rose, looking more like himself than since the previous Sunday. A quiet resolution was in his eyes and voice as he said:

"Elder Wheat has more right here than I have. I want 'o say that I'm going to give up my church in Douglass and"——A murmur broke out, which he silenced with his raised hand. "I find I don't believe any longer what I've been believing and preaching. Hold on! let me go on. I don't quite know where I'll bring up, but I think my religion will simmer down finally to about this: A full half-bushel to the half-bushel and sixteen ounces to the pound." Here two or three cheered. "Do unto others as you'd have others do unto you." Applause from several, quickly suppressed as the speaker went on, Elder Wheat listening as if petrified, with his mouth open.

"I'm going out of preaching, at least for the present. After things get into shape with me again, I may set up to teach people how to live, but just now I can't do it. I've got all I can do to instruct myself. Just one thing more. I owe two or three of you here. I've got the money for William Bacon, James Bartlett and John Jennings. I turn the mare and cutter over to Jacob Bensen, for the note he holds. I hain't got much religion left, but I've got some morality. That's all I want to say now."

When he sat down there was a profound hush; then Bacon arose.

"That's *man's* talk, that is! An' I jest want 'o say, Andrew Pill, that you kin jest forget you owe me anything. An' if ye want any help come to me. Y're jest gittun' ready to preach, 'n' I'm ready to give ye my support."

"That's the talk," said Councill. "I'm with ye on that."

Pill shook his head. The painful silence which followed was broken by the effusive voice of Wheat:

"Let us pray—and remember our lost brother."

The urgings of the people were of no avail. Mr. Pill settled up his affairs, and moved to Cresco, where he went back into trade with a friend, and for three years attended silently to his customers, lived down their curiosity and studied anew the problem of life. Then he moved away, and no one knew whither.

One day, last year, Bacon met Jennings on the road.

"Heerd anything o' Pill lately?"

"No; have you?"

"Waal, yes. Brown told me he ran acrost him down in Eelinoy, doun' well, too."

"In dry goods?"

"No, preachun'."

"Preachun'?"

"So Brown said. Kind of a free-f'r-all church, I reckon from what Jedge told me. Built a new church, fills it twice a Sunday. I'd like to hear him, but he's got t' be too big a gun f'r us. Ben studyun', they say; went t' school."

Jennings drove sadly and thoughtfully on.

"Rather stumps Brother Jennings," laughed Bacon, in his leonine fashion.

Part III.

WILLIAM BACON'S HIRED MAN: AND DAUGHTER MARIETTA.

... Love and youth pass swiftly: Love sings,
And April's sun fans warmer sunlight from his wings.

WILLIAM BACON'S MAN

I.

THE yellow March sun lay powerfully on the bare Iowa prairie, where the plowed fields were already turning warm and brown, and only here and there in a corner or on the north side of the fence did the sullen drifts remain, and they were so dark and low that they hardly appeared to break the mellow brown of the fields.

There passed also an occasional flock of geese, cheerful harbingers of spring, and the prairie-chickens had set up their morning symphony, wide-swelling, wonderful with its prophecy of the new birth of grass and grain and the springing life of all breathing things. The crow passed now and then, uttering his resonant croak, but the crane had not yet sent forth his bugle note.

Lyman Gilman rested on his ax-helve at the wood-pile of Farmer Bacon to listen to the music around him. In a vague way he was powerfully moved by it. He heard the hens singing their weird, raucous, monotonous song, and saw them burrowing in the dry chip-dust near him. He saw the young colts and cattle frisking in the sunny space around the straw-stacks, absorbed through his bare arms and uncovered head the heat of the sun, and felt the soft wooing of the air so deeply that he broke into an unwonted exclamation:

"Glory! we'll be seeding by Friday, sure."

This short and disappointing soliloquy was, after all, an expression of deep emotion. To the Western farmer the very word "seeding" is a poem. And these few words, coming from Lyman Gilman, meant more and expressed more than many a large and ambitious spring-time song.

But the glory of all the slumbrous landscape, the stately beauty of the sky with its masses of fleecy vapor, were swept away by the sound of a girl's voice humming, "Come to the Savior," while she bustled about the kitchen near by. The windows were open. Ah! what suggestion to these dwellers in a rigorous climate was in the first unsealing of the windows! How sweet it was to the pale and weary women after their long imprisonment!

As Lyman sat down on his maple log to hear better, a plump face appeared at the window, and a clear girl-voice said:

"Smell anything, Lime?"

He snuffed the air. "Cookies, by the great horn spoons!" he yelled, leaping up. "Bring me some, an' see me eat; it'll do ye good."

"Come an' get 'm," laughed the face at the window.

"Oh, it's nicer out here, Merry Etty. What's the rush? Bring me out some, an' set down on this log."

With a nod Marietta disappeared, and soon came out with a plate of cookies in one hand and a cup of milk in the other.

"Poor little man, he's all tired out, ain't he?"

Lime, taking the cue, collapsed in a heap, and said feebly, "Bread, bread!"

"Won't milk an' cookies do as well?"

He brushed off the log and motioned her to sit down beside him, but she hesitated a little and colored a little.

"O Lime, s'pose somebody should see us?"

"Let 'em. What in thunder do we care? Sit down an' gimme a holt o' them cakes. I'm just about done up. I couldn't 'a' stood it another minute."

She sat down beside him with a laugh and a pretty blush. She was in her apron, and the sleeves of her dress were rolled to her elbows, displaying the strong, round arms. Wholesome and sweet she looked and smelled, the scent of the cooking round her. Lyman munched a couple of the cookies and gulped a pint of milk before he spoke.

"Whadda we care who sees us sittin' side b' side? Ain't we goin' t' be married soon?"

"Oh, them cookies in the oven!" she shrieked, leaping up and running to the house. She looked back as she reached the kitchen door, however, and smiled with a flushed face. Lime slapped his knee and roared with laughter at his bold stroke.

"Ho! ho!" he laughed. "Didn't I do it slick? Ain't nothin' green in *my* eye, I guess." In an intense and pleasurable abstraction he finished the cookies and the milk. Then he yelled:

"Hey! Merry—Merry Etty!"

"Whadda ye want?" sang the girl from the window, her face still rosy with confusion.

"Come out here and git these things."

The girl shook her head, with a laugh.

"Come out an' git 'm, 'r by jingo I'll throw 'em at ye! Come on, now!"

The girl looked at the huge, handsome fellow, the sun falling on his golden hair and beard, and came slowly out to him—came creeping along with her hand outstretched for the plate which Lime, with a laugh in his sunny blue eyes, extended at the full length of his bare arm. The girl made a snatch at it, but his left hand caught her by the wrist, and away went cup and plate as he drew her to him and kissed her in spite of her struggles.

"My! ain't you strong!" she said, half-ruefully and half-admiringly, as she shrugged her shoulders. "If you'd use a little more o' *that* choppin' wood, Dad wouldn't 'a' lost s' much money by yeh."

Lime grew grave.

"There's the hog in the fence, Merry; what's yer dad goin' t' say"——

"About what?"

"About our gitt'n' married this spring."

"I guess you'd better find out what *I'm* a-goin' t' say, Lime Gilman, 'fore you pitch into Dad."

"I *know* what you're a-goin' t' say."

"No, y' don't."

"Yes, but I *do*, though."

"Well, ask me, and see, if you think you're so smart. Jest as like 's not, you'll slip up."

"All right; here goes. Marietty Bacon, ain't you an' Lime Gilman goin' t' be married?"

"No, sir, we ain't," laughed the girl, snatching up the plate and darting away to the house, where she struck up "Weevily Wheat," and went busily on about her cooking. Lime threw a kiss at her, and fell to work on his log with startling energy.

Lyman looked forward to his interview with the old man with as much trepidation as he had ever known, though commonly he had little fear of anything—but a girl.

Marietta was not only the old man's only child, his housekeeper, his wife having at last succumbed to the ferocious toil of the farm. It was reasonable to suppose, therefore, that he would surrender his claim on the girl reluctantly. Rough as he was, he loved Marietta strongly, and would find it exceedingly hard to get along without her.

Lyman mused on these things as he drove the gleaming ax into the huge maple logs. He was something more than the usual hired man, being a lumberman from the Wisconsin pineries, where he had sold out his interest in a camp not three weeks before the day he began work for Bacon. He had a nice "little wad o' money" when he left the camp and started for La Crosse, but he had been robbed in his hotel the first night in the city, and was left nearly penniless. It was a great blow to him, for, as he said, every cent of that money "stood fer hard knocks an' poor feed. When I smelt of it I could jest see the cold, frosty mornin's and the late nights. I could feel the hot sun on my back like it was when I worked in the harvest-field. By jingo! It kind o' made my toes curl up."

But he went resolutely out to work again, and here he was chopping wood in old man Bacon's yard, thinking busily on the talk which had just passed between him and Marietta.

"By jingo!" he said all at once, stopping short, with the ax on his shoulder. "If I hadn't 'a' been robbed I wouldn't 'a' come here—I never'd metMerry. Thunder and jimson root! Wasn't that a narrow escape?"

And then he laughed so heartily that the girl looked out of the window again to see what in the world he was doing. He had his hat in his hand and was whacking his thigh with it.

"Lyman Gilman, what in the world ails you to-day? It's perfectly ridiculous the way you yell and talk t' y'rself out there on the chips. You beat the hens, I declare if you don't."

Lime put on his hat and walked up to the window, and, resting his great bare arms on the sill, and his chin on his arms, said:

"Merry, I'm goin' to tackle 'Dad' this afternoon. He'll be settin' up the new seeder, and I'm goin' t' climb right on the back of his neck. He's jest *got* t' give me a chance."

Marietta looked sober in sympathy.

"Well! P'raps it's best to have it over with, Lime, but someway I feel kind o' scary about it."

Lime stood for a long time looking in at the window, watching the light-footed girl as she set the table in the middle of the sun-lighted kitchen floor. The kettle hissed, the meat sizzled, sending up a delicious odor; a hen stood in the open door and sang a sort of cheery half-human song, while to and fro moved the sweet-faced, lithe and powerful girl, followed by the smiling eyes at the window.

"Merry, you look purty as a picture. You look just like the wife I be'n a-huntin' for all these years, sure 's shootin'."

Marietta colored with pleasure.

"Does Dad pay you to stand an' look at me an' say pretty things t' the cook?"

"No, he don't. But I'm willin' t' do it without pay. I could jest stand here till kingdom come an' look at you. Hello! I hear a wagon. I guess I better hump into that wood-pile."

"I think so, too. Dinner's most ready, and Dad 'll be here soon."

Lime was driving away furiously at a tough elm log when Farmer Bacon drove into the yard with a new seeder in his wagon. Lime whacked away busily while Bacon stabled the team, and in a short time Marietta called, in a long-drawn, musical fashion:

"Dinner-r-r!"

After sozzling their faces at the well the two men went in and sat down at the table. Bacon was not much of a talker at any time, and at mealtime, in seeding, eating was the main business in hand; therefore the meal was a silent one, Marietta and Lime not caring to talk on general topics. The hour was an anxious one for her, and an important one for him.

"Wal, now, Lime, seedun' 's the nex' thing," said Bacon, as he shoved back his chair and glared around from under his bushy eyebrows. "We can'tdo too much this afternoon. That seeder's got t' be set up an' a lot o' seed-wheat cleaned up. You unload the machine while I feed the pigs."

Lime sat still till the old man was heard outside calling "Oo-ee, poo-ee" to the pigs in the yard; then he smiled at Marietta, but she said:

"He's got on one of his fits, Lime; I don't b'lieve you'd better tackle him t'-day."

"Don't you worry; I'll fix him. Come, now, give me a kiss."

"Why, you great thing! You—took"——

"I know, but I want you to *give* 'em to me. Just walk right up to me an' give me a smack t' bind the bargain."

"I ain't made any bargain," laughed the girl. Then, feeling the force of his tender tone, she added: "Will you behave, and go right off to your work?"

"Jest like a little man—hope t' die!"

"*Lime!*" roared the old man from the barn.

"Hello!" replied Lime, grinning joyously and winking at the girl, as much as to say, "This would paralyze the old man if he saw it."

He went out to the shed where Bacon was at work, as serene as if he had not a fearful task on hand. He was apprehensive that the father might "gig back" unless rightly approached, and so he awaited a good opportunity.

The right moment seemed to present itself along about the middle of the afternoon. Bacon was down on the ground under the machine, tightening some burrs. This was a good chance for two reasons. In the first place the keen, almost savage eyes of Bacon were no longer where they could glare on him, and in spite of his cool exterior Lime had just as soon not have the old man looking at him.

Besides, the old farmer had been telling about his "river eighty," which was without a tenant; the man who had taken it, having lost his wife, had grown disheartened and had given it up.

"It's an almighty good chance for a man with a small family. Good house an' barn, good land. A likely young feller with a team an' a woman could do tip-top on that eighty. If he wanted more, I'd let him have an eighty j'inun'"——

"I'd like t' try that m'self," said Lime, as a feeler. The old fellow said nothing in reply for a moment.

"Ef you had a team an' tools an' a woman, I'd jest as lief you'd have it as anybody."

"Sell me your blacks, and I'll pay half down—the balance in the fall. I can pick up some tools, and as for a woman, Merry Etty an' me have talked that over to-day. She's ready to—ready to marry me whenever you say go."

There was an ominous silence under the seeder, as if the father could not believe his ears.

"What's—what's that?" he stuttered. "Who'd you say? What about Merry Etty?"

"She's agreed to marry me."

"The hell you say!" roared Bacon, as the truth burst upon him. "So that's what you do when I go off to town and leave you to chop wood. So you're goun' to git married, hey?"

He was now where Lime could see him, glaring up into his smiling blue eyes. Lime stood his ground.

"Yes, sir. That's the calculation."

"Well, I guess I'll have somethin' t' say about that," nodding his head violently.

"I rather expected y' would. Blaze away. Your privilege—my bad luck. Sail in, ol' man. What's y'r objection to me fer a son-in-law?"

"Don't you worry, young feller. I'll come at it soon enough," went on Bacon, as he turned up another burr in a very awkward corner. In his nervous excitement the wrench slipped, banging his knuckle.

"Ouch! Thunder—m-m-m!" howled and snarled the wounded man.

"What's the matter? Bark y'r knuckle?" queried Lime, feeling a mighty impulse to laugh. But when he saw the old savage straighten up and glare at him he sobered. Bacon was now in a frightful temper. The veins in his great, bare, weather-beaten neck swelled dangerously.

"Jest let me say right here that I've had enough o' you. You can't live on the same acre with my girl another day."

"What makes ye think I can't?" It was now the young man's turn to draw himself up, and as he faced the old man, his arms folded and each vast hand grasping an elbow, he looked like a statue of red granite, and the hands resembled the paws of a crouching lion; but his eyes smiled.

"I don't *think*, I know ye won't."

"What's the objection to me?"

"Objection? Hell! What's the inducement? My hired man, an' not three shirts to yer back!"

"That's another; I've got four. Say, old man, did you ever work out for a living?"

"That's none o' your business," growled Bacon, a little taken down. "I've worked, an' scraped, an' got t'gether a little prop'ty here, an' they ain't no sucker like you goun' to come 'long here, an' live off me, an' spend my prop'ty after I'm dead. You can jest bet high on that."

"Who's goin' t' live on ye?"

"You're aimun' to."

"I ain't, neither."

"Yes, y'are. You've loafed on me ever since I hired ye."

"That's a"——Lime checked himself for Marietta's sake, and the enraged father went on:

"I hired ye t' cut wood, an' you've gone an' fooled my daughter away from me. Now you jest figger up what I owe ye, and git out o' here. Ye can't go too soon t' suit *me*."

Bacon was renowned as the hardest man in Cedar County to handle, and though he was getting old, he was still a terror to his neighbors when roused. He was honest, temperate, and a good neighbor until something carried him off his balance; then he became as cruel as a panther and as savage as a grizzly. All this Lime knew, but it did not keep his anger down so much as did the thought of Marietta. His silence infuriated Bacon, who yelled hoarsely:

"Git out o' this!"

"Don't be in a rush, ol' man"——

Bacon hurled himself upon Lime, who threw out one hand and stopped him, while he said in a low voice:

"Stay right where you are, ol' man. I'm dangerous. It's for Merry's sake"———

The infuriated old man struck at him. Lime warded off the blow, and with a sudden wrench and twist threw him to the ground with frightful force. Before Bacon could rise, Marietta, who had witnessed the scene, came flying from the house.

"Lime! Father! What are you doing?"

"I—couldn't help it, Merry. It was him 'r me," said Lime, almost sadly.

"Dad, ain't you got no sense? What 're you thinking of? You jest stop right now. I won't have it."

He rose while she clung to him; he seemed a little dazed. It was the first time he had ever been thrown, and he could not but feel a certain respect for his opponent, but he could not give way.

"Pack up yer duds," he snarled, "an' git off'n my land. I'll have the money fer ye when ye come back. I'll give ye jest five minutes to git clear o' here. Merry, you stay here."

The young man saw it was useless to remain, as it would only excite the old man; and so, with a look of apology, not without humor, at Marietta, he went to the house to get his valise. The girl wept silently while the father raged up and down. His mood frightened her.

"I thought you had more sense than t' take up with such a dirty houn'."

"He ain't a houn'," she blazed forth, "and he's just as good and clean as you are."

"Shut up! Don't let me hear another word out o' your head. I'm boss here yet, I reckon."

Lime came out with his valise in his hand.

"Good-by, Merry," he said cheerily. She started to go to him, but her father's rough grasp held her.

"Set *down*, an' stay there."

Lime was going out of the gate.

"Here! Come and get y'r money," yelled the old man, extending some bills. "Here's twenty"———-

"Go to thunder with your money," retorted Lime. "I've had my pay for my month's work." As he said that, he thought of the sunny kitchen and the merry girl, and his throat choked. Good-by to the sweet girl whose smile was so much to him, and to the happy noons and nights her eyes had made for him. He waved his hat at her as he stood in the open gate, and the sun lighted his handsome head into a sort of glory in her eyes. Then he turned and walked rapidly off down the road, not looking back.

The girl, when she could no longer see him, dashed away, and, sobbing violently, entered the house.

II.

THERE was just a suspicion of light in the east, a mere hint of a glow, when Lyman walked cautiously around the corner of the house and tapped at Marietta's window. She was sleeping soundly and did not hear, for she had been restless during the first part of the night. He tapped again, and the girl woke without knowing what woke her.

Lyman put the blade of his pocket-knife under the window and raised it a little, and then placed his lips to the crack, and spoke in a sepulchral tone, half groan, half whisper:

"Merry! Merry Etty!"

The dazed girl sat up in bed and listened, while her heart almost stood still.

"Merry, it's me—Lime. Come to the winder." The girl hesitated, and Lyman spoke again.

"Come, I hain't got much time. This is your last chance t' see me. It's now 'r never."

The girl slipped out of bed and, wrapping herself in a shawl, crept to the window.

"Boost on that winder," commanded Lyman. She raised it enough to admit his head, which came just above the sill; then she knelt on the floor by the window.

Her eyes stared wide and dark.

"Lime, what in the world do you mean"——

"I mean business," he replied. "I ain't no last year's chicken; I know when the old man sleeps the soundest." He chuckled pleasantly.

"How 'd y' fool old Rove?"

"Never mind about that now; they's something more important on hand. You've got t' go with me."

She drew back. "Oh, Lime, I can't!"

He thrust a great arm in and caught her by the wrist.

"Yes, y' can. This is y'r last chance. If I go off without ye t'-night, I never come back. What make ye gig back? Are ye 'fraid o' me?"

"N-no; but—but"——

"But what, Merry Etty?"

"It ain't right to go an' leave Dad all alone. Where y' goin' t' take me, anyhow?"

"Milt Jennings let me have his horse an' buggy; they're down the road a piece, an' we'll go right down to Rock River and be married by sun-up."

The girl still hesitated, her firm, boyish will unwontedly befogged. Resolute as she was, she could not at once accede to his demand.

"Come, make up your mind soon. The old man 'll fill me with buck-shot if he catches sight o' me." He drew her arm out of the window and laid his bearded cheek to it. "Come, little one, we're made for each other; God knows it. Come! It's him 'r me."

The girl's head dropped, consented.

"That's right! Now a kiss to bind the bargain. There! What, cryin'? No more o' that, little one. Now I'll give you jest five minutes to git on your Sunday-go-t'-meetin' clo'es. Quick, there goes a rooster. It's gittin' white in the east."

The man turned his back to the window and gazed at the western sky with a wealth of unuttered and unutterable exultation in his heart. Far off a rooster gave a long, clear blast—would it be answered in the barn? Yes; some wakeful ear had caught it, and now came the answer, but faint, muffled and drowsy. The dog at his feet whined uneasily as if suspecting something wrong. The wind from the south was full of the wonderful odor of springing grass, warm, brown earth, and oozing sap. Overhead, to the west, the stars were shining in the cloudless sky, dimmed a little in brightness by the faint silvery veil of moisture in the air. The man's soul grew very tender as he stood waiting for his bride. He was rough, illiterate, yet there was something fine about him after all, a kind of simplicity and a gigantic, leonine tenderness.

He heard his sweetheart moving about inside, and thought: "The old man won't hold out when he finds we're married. He can't get along without her. If he does, why, I'll rent a farm here, and we'll go to work housekeepin'. I can git the money. She sha'n't always be poor," he ended, with a vow.

The window was raised again, and the girl's voice was heard low and tremulous:

"Lime, I'm ready, but I wish we didn't"——

He put his arm around her waist and helped her out, and did not put her down till they reached the road. She was completely dressed, even to her hat and shoes, but she mourned:

"My hair is every-which-way; Lime, how can I be married so?"

They were nearing the horse and buggy now, and Lime laughed. "Oh, we'll stop at Jennings's and fix up. Milt knows what's up, and has told his mother by this time. So just laugh as jolly as you can."

Soon they were in the buggy, the impatient horse swung into the road at a rattling pace, and as Marietta leaned back in the seat, thinking of what she had done, she cried lamentably, in spite of all the caresses and pleadings of her lover.

But the sun burst up from the plain, the prairie-chickens took up their mighty chorus on the hills, robins met them on the way, flocks of wild geese, honking cheerily, drove far overhead toward the north, and, with these sounds of a golden spring day in her ears, the bride grew cheerful, and laughed.

III.

AT about the time the sun was rising, Farmer Bacon, roused from his sleep by the crowing of the chickens on the dry knolls in the fields as well as by those in the barnyard, rolled out of bed wearily, wondering why he should feel so drowsy. Then he remembered the row with Lime and his subsequent inability to sleep with thinking over it. There was a dull pain in his breast, which made him uncomfortable.

As was his usual custom, he went out into the kitchen and built the fire for Marietta, filled the tea-kettle with water, and filled the water-bucket in the sink. Then he went to her bed-room door and knocked with his knuckles as he had done for years in precisely the same fashion.

Rap—rap—rap. "Hello, Merry! Time t' git up. Broad daylight, an' birds a-singun'."

Without waiting for an answer he went out to the barn and worked away at his chores. He took such delight in the glorious morning and the turbulent life of the farmyard that his heart grew light and he hummed a tune which sounded like the merry growl of a lion. "Poo-ee, poo-ee," he called to the pigs as they swarmed across the yard.

"Ahrr! you big, fat rascals, them hams o' yourn is clear money. One of ye shall go t' buy Merry a new dress," he said as he glanced at the house and saw the smoke pouring out the stove-pipe. "Merry 's a good girl; she's stood by her old pap when other girls 'u'd 'a' gone back on 'im."

While currying horses he went all over the ground of the quarrel yesterday, and he began to see it in a different light. He began to see that Lyman was a good man and an able man, and that his own course was a foolish one.

"When I git mad," he confessed to himself, "I don't know anythin'. But I won't give her up. She ain't old 'nough t' marry yet—and, besides, I need her."

After finishing his chores, as usual, he went to the well and washed his face and hands, then entered the kitchen—to find the tea-kettle boiling over, and no signs of breakfast anywhere, and no sign of the girl.

"Well, I guess she felt sleepy this mornin'. Poor gal! Mebbe she cried half the night."

"Merry!" he called, gently, at the door. "Merry, m' gal! Pap needs his breakfast."

There was no reply, and the old man's face stiffened into a wild surprise. He knocked heavily again and got no reply, and, with a white face and shaking hand, he flung the door open and gazed at the empty bed. His hand dropped to his side; his head turned slowly from the bed to the open window; he rushed forward and looked out on the ground, where he saw the tracks of a man.

He fell heavily into the chair by the bed, while a deep groan broke from his stiff and twitching lips.

"She's left me! She's left me!"

For a long half-hour the iron-muscled old man sat there motionless, hearing not the songs of the hens or the birds far out in the brilliant sunshine. He had lost sight of his farm, his day's work, and felt no hunger for food. He did not doubt that her going was final. He felt that she was gone from him forever. If she ever came back it would not be as his daughter, but as the wife of Gilman. She had deserted him, fled in the night like a thief; his heart began to harden again, and he rose stiffly. His native stubbornness began to assert itself, the first great shock over, and he went out to the kitchen, and prepared, as best he could, a breakfast, and sat down to it. In some way his appetite failed him, and he fell to thinking over his past life, of the death of his wife, and the early death of his only boy. He was still trying to think what his life would be in the future without his girl, when two carriages drove into the yard. It was about the middle of the forenoon, and the prairie-chickens had ceased to boom and squawk; in fact, that was why he knew that he had been sitting two hours at the table. Before he could rise he heard swift feet and a merry voice. Then Marietta burst through the door.

"Hello, Pap! How you makin' out with break"——She saw a look on his face that went to her heart like a knife. She saw a lonely and deserted old man sitting at his cold and cheerless breakfast, and with a remorseful cry she ran across the floor and took him in her arms, kissing him again and again, while Mr. John Jennings and his wife stood in the door.

"Poor ol' Pap! Merry couldn't leave you. She's come back to stay as long as he lives."

The old man remained cold and stern. His deep voice had a raucous note in it as he pushed her away from him, noticing no one else.

"But how do you come back t' me?"

The girl grew rosy, but she stood proudly up.

"I come back a wife of a *man*, Pap; a wife like my mother, an' this t' hang beside hers;" and she laid down a rolled piece of parchment.

"Take it an' go," growled he; "take yer lazy lubber an' git out o' my sight. I raised ye, took keer o' ye when ye was little, sent ye t' school, bought ye dresses,—done everythin' for ye I could, 'lowin' t' have ye stand by me when I got old,—but no, ye must go back on yer ol' pap, an' go off in the night with a good-f'r-nothin' houn' that nobuddy knows anything about—a feller that never done a thing fer ye in the world"——

"What did you do for mother that she left *her* father and mother and went with you? How much did you have when you took her away from her good home an' brought her away out here among the wolves an' Indians? I've heard you an' her say a hundred times that you didn't have a chair in the house. Now, why do you talk so t' me when I want t' git—when Lime comes and asks for me?"

The old man was staggered. He looked at the smiling face of John Jennings and the tearful face of Mrs. Jennings, who had returned with Lyman. But his face hardened again as he caught sight of Lime looking in at him. His absurd pride would not let him relent. Lime saw it, and stepped forward.

"Ol' man, I want t' take a little inning now. I'm a fair, square man. I asked ye fer Merry as a man should. I told you I'd had hard luck, when I first came here. I had five thousand dollars in clean cash stole from me. I hain't got a thing now except credit, but that's good fer enough t' stock a little farm with. Now, I wan' to be fair and square in this thing. You wan' to rent a farm; I need one. Let me have the river eighty, or I'll take the whole business on a share of a third an' Merry Etty, and I to stay here with you jest as if nothin' 'd happened. Come, now, what d' y' say?"

There was something winning in the whole bearing of the man as he stood before the father, who remained silent and grim.

"Or if you don't do that, why, there's nothin' left fer Merry an' me but to go back to La Crosse, where I can have my choice of a dozen farms. Now this is the way things is standin'. I don't want to be underhanded about this thing"——

"That's a fair offer," said Mr. Jennings in the pause which followed. "You'd better do it, neighbor Bacon. Nobuddy need know how things stood; they were married in my house—I thought that 'u'd be best. You can't live without your girl," he went on, "any more 'n I could without my boy. You'd better"——

The figure at the table straightened up. Under his tufted eyebrows his keen gray eyes flashed from one to the other. His hands knotted.

"Go slow!" went on the smooth voice of Jennings, known all the country through as a peace-maker. "Take time t' think it over. Stand out, an' you'll live here alone without chick 'r child; give in, and this house 'll bubble over with noise and young ones. Now is short, and forever's a long time to feel sorry in."

The old man at the table knitted his eyebrows, and a distorted, quivering, ghastly smile broke out on his face. His chest heaved; then he burst forth:

"Gal, yank them gloves off, an' git me something to eat—breakfus 'r dinner, I don't care which. Lime, you infernal idiot, git out there and gear up them horses. What in thunder you foolun' around about hyere in seed'n'? Come, hustle, all o' ye!"

And then they shouted in laughter, while the cause of it all strode unsteadily but resolutely out toward the barn, followed by the bridegroom, who was laughing—silently.

Part IV.

SIM BURNS'S WIFE
A PRAIRIE HEROINE.

A tale of toil that's never done I tell;
Of life where love's a fleeting wing
Above the woman's hopeless hell
Of ceaseless, year-round journeying.

SIM BURNS'S WIFE.

I.

LUCRETIA BURNS had never been handsome, even in her days of early girlhood, and now she was middle-aged, distorted with work and child-bearing, and looking faded and worn as one of the boulders that lay beside the pasture fence near where she sat milking a large white cow.

She had no shawl or hat and no shoes, for it was still muddy in the little yard, where the cattle stood patiently fighting the flies and mosquitoes swarming into their skins, already wet with blood. The evening was oppressive with its heat, and a ring of just-seen thunder-heads gave premonitions of an approaching storm.

She rose from the cow's side at last, and, taking her pails of foaming milk, staggered toward the gate. The two pails hung from her lean arms, her bare feet slipped on the filthy ground, her greasy and faded calico dress showed her tired, swollen ankles, and the mosquitoes swarmed mercilessly on her neck and bedded themselves in her colorless hair.

The children were quarreling at the well, and the sound of blows could be heard. Calves were querulously calling for their milk, and little turkeys, lost in a tangle of grass, were piping plaintively.

The sun just setting struck through a long, low rift like a boy peeping beneath the eaves of a huge roof. Its light brought out Lucretia's face as she leaned her sallow forehead on the top bar of the gate and looked toward the west.

It was a pitifully worn, almost tragic face—long, thin, sallow, hollow-eyed. The mouth had long since lost the power to shape itself into a kiss, and had a droop at the corners which seemed to announce a breaking-down at any moment into a despairing wail. The collarless neck and sharp shoulders showed painfully.

She felt vaguely that the night was beautiful. The setting sun, the noise of frogs, the nocturnal insects beginning to pipe—all in some way called her girlhood back to her, though there was little in her girlhood to give her pleasure. Her large gray eyes grew round, deep and wistful as she saw the illimitable craggy clouds grow crimson, roll slowly up, and fire at the top. A childish scream recalled her.

"Oh, my soul!" she half groaned, half swore, as she lifted her milk and hurried to the well. Arriving there, she cuffed the children right and left with all her remaining strength, saying in justification:

"My soul! can't you—you young 'uns give me a minute's peace? Land knows, I'm almost gone up; washin', an' milkin' six cows, and tendin' you, and cookin' fr *him*, ought 'o be enough fr one day! Sadie, you let him drink now 'r I'll slap your head off, you hateful thing! Why can't you behave, when you know I'm jest about dead?" She was weeping now, with nervous weakness. "Where's y'r pa?" she asked after a moment, wiping her eyes with her apron.

One of the group, the one cuffed last, sniffed out, in rage and grief:

"He's in the cornfield; where'd ye s'pose he was?"

"Good land! why don't the man work all night? Sile, you put that dipper in that milk agin, an' I'll whack you till your head'll swim! Sadie, le' go Pet, an' go 'n get them turkeys out of the grass 'fore it gits dark! Bob, you go tell y'r dad if he wants the rest o' them cows milked he's got 'o do it himself. I jest can't, and what's more, I *won't*," she ended, rebelliously.

Having strained the milk and fed the children, she took some skimmed milk from the cans and started to feed the calves bawling strenuously behind the barn. The eager and unruly brutes pushed and struggled to get into the pails all at once, and in consequence spilt nearly all of the milk on the ground. This was the last trial; the woman fell down on the damp grass and moaned and sobbed like a crazed thing. The children came to seek her and stood around like little partridges, looking at her in scared silence, till at last the little one began to wail. Then the mother rose wearily to her feet, and walked slowly back toward the house.

She heard Burns threshing his team at the well, with the sound of oaths. He was tired, hungry and ill-tempered, but she was too desperate to care. His poor, overworked team did not move quickly enough for him, and his extra long turn in the corn had made him dangerous. His eyes gleamed wrathfully from his dust-laid face.

"Supper ready?" he growled.

"Yes, two hours ago."

"Well, I can't help it!" he said, understanding her reproach. "That devilish corn is gettin' too tall to plow again, and I've got 'o go through it to-morrow or not at all. Cows milked?"

"Part of 'em."

"How many left?"

"Three."

"Hell! Which three?"

"Spot, and Brin, and Cherry."

"*Of* course, left the three worst ones. I'll be damned if I milk a cow to-night. I don't see why you play out jest the nights I need ye most." Here he kicked a child out of the way. "Git out o' that! Hain't you got no sense? I'll learn ye"——

"Stop that, Sim Burns," cried the woman, snatching up the child. "You're a reg'lar ol' hyeny,—that's what you are," she added defiantly, roused at last from her lethargy.

"You're a—beauty, that's what *you* are," he said, pitilessly. "Keep your brats out f'um under my feet." And he strode off to a barn after his team, leaving her with a fierce hate in her heart. She heard him yelling at his team in their stalls: "Git around there, damn yeh."

The children had had their supper; so she took them to bed. She was unusually tender to them, for she wanted to make up in some way for her previous harshness. The ferocity of her husband had shown up her own petulant temper hideously, and she sat and sobbed in the darkness a long time beside the cradle where little Pet slept.

She heard Burns come growling in and tramp about, but she did not rise. The supper was on the table; he could wait on himself. There was an awful feeling at her heart as she sat there and the house grew quiet. She thought of suicide in a vague way; of somehow taking her children in her arms and sinking into a lake somewhere, where she would never more be troubled, where she could sleep forever, without toil or hunger.

Then she thought of the little turkeys wandering in the grass, of the children sleeping at last, of the quiet, wonderful stars. Then she thought of the cows left unmilked, and listened to them stirring uneasily in the yard. She rose, at last, and stole forth. She could not rid herself of the thought that they would suffer. She knew what the dull ache in the full breasts of a mother was, and she could not let them stand at the bars all night moaning for relief.

The mosquitoes had gone, but the frogs and katydids still sang, while over in the west Venus shone. She was a long time milking the cows; her hands were so tired she had often to stop and rest them, while the tears fell unheeded into the pail. She saw and felt little of the external as she sat there. She thought in vague retrospect of how sweet it seemed the first time Sim came to see her; of the many rides to town with him when he was an accepted lover; of the few things he had given her—a coral breastpin and a ring.

She felt no shame at her present miserable appearance; she was past personal pride. She hardly felt as if the tall, strong girl, attractive with health and hope, could be the same soul as the woman who now sat in utter despair listening to the heavy breathing of the happy cows, grateful for the relief from their burden of milk.

She contrasted her lot with that of two or three women that she knew (not a very high standard), who kept hired help, and who had fine houses of four or five rooms. Even the neighbors were better off than she, for they didn't have such quarrels. But she wasn't to blame—Sim didn't—— Then her mind changed to a dull resentment against "things." Everything seemed against her.

She rose at last and carried her second load of milk to the well, strained it, washed out the pails, and, after bathing her tired feet in a tub that stood there, she put on a pair of horrible shoes, without stockings, and crept stealthily into the house. Sim did not hear her as she slipped up the stairs to the little low, unfinished chamber beside her oldest children. She could not bear to sleep near *him* that night,—she wanted a chance to sob herself to quiet.

As for Sim, he was a little disturbed, but would as soon have cut off his head as acknowledge himself in the wrong. As he went to bed, and found her still away, he yelled up the stairway:

"Say, o' woman, ain't ye comin' to bed?" Upon receiving no answer he rolled his aching body into the creaking bed. "Do as y' damn please about it. If y' want to sulk y' can." And in such wise the family grew quiet in sleep, while the moist, warm air pulsed with the ceaseless chime of the crickets.

II.

WHEN Sim Burns woke the next morning he felt a sharper twinge of remorse. It was not a broad or well-defined feeling—just a sense that he had been unduly irritable, not that on the whole he was not in the right. Little Pet lay with the warm June sunshine filling his baby eyes, curiously content in striking at flies that buzzed around his little mouth.

The man thrust his dirty, naked feet into his huge boots, and, without washing his face or combing his hair, went out to the barn to do his chores.

He was a type of the average prairie farmer, and his whole surrounding was typical of the time. He had a quarter-section of fine level land, bought with incredible toil, but his house was a little box-like structure, costing, perhaps, five hundred dollars. It had three rooms and the ever-present summer kitchen attached to the back. It was unpainted and had no touch of beauty—a mere box.

His stable was built of slabs and banked and covered with straw. It looked like a den, was low and long, and had but one door in the end. The cow-yard held ten or fifteen cattle of various kinds, while a few calves were bawling from a pen near by. Behind the barn, on the west and north, was a fringe of willows forming a "wind-break." A few broken and discouraged fruit trees standing here and there among the weeds formed the garden. In short, he was spoken of by his neighbors as "a hard-working cuss, and tol'ably well fixed."

No grace had come or ever could come into his life. Back of him were generations of men like himself, whose main business had been to work hard, live miserably, and beget children to take their places when they died.

His courtship had been delayed so long on account of poverty that it brought little of humanizing emotion into his life. He never mentioned his love-life now, or if he did, it was only to sneer obscenely at it. He had long since ceased to kiss his wife or even speak kindly to her. There was no longer any sanctity to life or love. He chewed tobacco and toiled on from year to year without any very clearly defined idea of the future. His life was mainly regulated from without.

He was tall, dark and strong, in a flat-chested, slouching sort of way, and had grown neglectful of even decency in his dress. He wore the American farmer's customary outfit of rough brown pants, hickory shirt and greasy wool hat. It differed from his neighbors' mainly in being a little dirtier and more ragged. His grimy hands were broad and strong as the clutch of a bear, and he was a "terrible feller to turn off work," as Councill said. "I 'druther have Sim Burns work for me one day than some men three. He's a linger." He worked with unusual speed this morning, and ended by milking all the cows himself as a sort of savage penance for his misdeeds the previous evening, muttering in self-defense:

"Seems 's if ever' cussid thing piles on to me at once. That corn, the road-tax, and hayin' comin' on, and now *she* gits her back up"——

When he went back to the well he sloshed himself thoroughly in the horse-trough and went to the house. He found breakfast ready, but his wife was not in sight. The older children were clamoring around the uninviting breakfast table, spread with cheap ware and with boiled potatoes and fried salt pork as the principal dishes.

"Where's y'r ma?" he asked, with a threatening note in his voice, as he sat down by the table.

"She's in the bed-room."

He rose and pushed open the door. The mother sat with the babe in her lap, looking out of the window down across the superb field of timothy, moving like a lake of purple water. She did not look around. She only grew rigid. Her thin neck throbbed with the pulsing of blood to her head.

"What's got into you *now?*" he said, brutally. "Don't be a fool. Come out and eat breakfast with me, an' take care o' y'r young ones."

She neither moved nor made a sound. With an oath he turned on his heel and went out to the table. Eating his breakfast in his usual wolfish fashion, he went out into the hot sun with his team and riding-plow, not a little disturbed by this new phase of his wife's "cantankerousness." He plowed steadily and sullenly all the forenoon, in the terrific heat and dust. The air was full of tempestuous threats, still and sultry, one of those days when work is a punishment. When he came in at noon he found things the same—dinner on the table, but his wife out in the garden with the youngest child.

"I c'n stand it as long as *she* can," he said to himself, in the hearing of the children, as he pushed back from the table and went back to work.

When he had finished the field of corn it was after sundown, and he came up to the house, hot, dusty, his shirt wringing wet with sweat, and his neck aching with the work of looking down all day at the corn-rows. His mood was still stern. The multitudinous lift, and stir, and sheen of the wide, green field had been lost upon him.

"I wonder if she's milked them cows," he muttered to himself. He gave a sigh of relief to find she had. But she had done so not for his sake, but for the sake of the poor, patient dumb brutes.

When he went to the bed-room after supper, he found that the cradle and his wife's few little boxes and parcels—poor, pathetic properties!—had been removed to the garret, which they called a chamber, and he knew he was to sleep alone again.

"She'll git over it, I guess." He was very tired, but he didn't feel quite comfortable enough to sleep. The air was oppressive. His shirt, wet in places, and stiff with dust in other places, oppressed him more than usual; so he rose and removed it, getting a clean one out of a drawer. This was an unusual thing for him, for he usually slept in the same shirt which he wore in his day's work; but it was Saturday night, and he felt justified in the extravagance.

In the meanwhile poor Lucretia was brooding over her life in a most dangerous fashion. All she had done and suffered for Simeon Burns came back to her till she wondered how she had endured it all. All day long in the midst of the glorious summer landscape she brooded.

"I hate him," she thought, with a fierce blazing up through the murk of her musing. "I hate t' live. But they ain't no hope. I'm tied down. I can't leave the children, and I ain't got no money. I couldn't make a living out in the world. I ain't never seen anything an' don't know anything."

She was too simple and too unknowing to speculate on the loss of her beauty, which would have brought her competency once—if sold in the right market. As she lay in her little attic bed, she was still sullenly thinking, wearily thinking of her life. She thought of a poor old horse which Sim had bought once, years before, and put to the plough when it was too old and weak to work. She could see her again as in a vision, that poor old mare, with sad head drooping, toiling, toiling, till at last she could no longer move, and lying down under the harness in the furrow, groaned under the whip—and died.

Then she wondered if her own numbness and despair meant death, and she held her breath to think harder upon it. She concluded at last, grimly, that she didn't care—only for the children.

The air was frightfully close in the little attic, and she heard the low mutter of the rising storm in the west. She forgot her troubles a little, listening to the far-off gigantic footsteps of the tempest.

Boom, boom, boom, it broke nearer and nearer, as if a vast cordon of cannon was being drawn around the horizon. Yet she was conscious only of pleasure. She had no fear. At last came the sweep of cool, fragrant storm-wind, a short and sudden dash of rain, and then, in the cool, sweet hush which followed, the worn and weary woman fell into a deep sleep.

III.

WHEN she woke the younger children were playing about on the floor in their night-clothes, and little Pet was sitting in a square of sunshine, intent on one of his shoes. He was too young to know how poor and squalid his surroundings were—the patch of sunshine flung on the floor glorified it all. He—little animal—was happy.

The poor of the Western prairies lie almost as unhealthily close together as do the poor of the city tenements. In the small hut of the peasant there is as little chance to escape close and tainting contact as in the coops and dens of the North End of proud Boston. In the midst of oceans of land, floods of sunshine and gulfs of verdure, the farmer lives in two or three small rooms. Poverty's eternal cordon is ever round the poor.

"Ma, why didn't you sleep with Pap last night?" asked Bob, the seven-year-old, when he saw she was awake at last. She flushed a dull red.

"You hush, will yeh? Because—I—it was too warm—and there was a storm comin'. You never mind askin' such questions. Is he gone out?"

"Yup. I heerd him callin' the pigs. It's Sunday, ain't it, ma?"

The fact seemed to startle her.

"Why, yes, so it is! Wal! Now, Sadie, you jump up an' dress quick 's y' can, an' Bob an' Sile, you run down an' bring s'm' water," she commanded, in nervous haste, beginning to dress. In the middle of the room there was scarce space to stand beneath the rafters.

When Sim came in for his breakfast he found it on the table, but his wife was absent.

"Where's y'r ma?" he asked, with a little less of the growl in his voice.

"She's upstairs with Pet."

The man ate his breakfast in dead silence, till at last Bob ventured to say:

"What makes ma ac' so?"

"Shut up!" was the brutal reply. The children began to take sides with the mother—all but the oldest girl, who was ten years old. To her the father turned now for certain things to be done, treating her in his rough fashion as a housekeeper, and the girl felt flattered and docile accordingly.

They were pitiably clad; like many farm-children, indeed, they could hardly be said to be clad at all. Sadie had on but two garments, a sort of undershirt of cotton and a faded calico dress, out of which her bare, yellow little legs protruded, lamentably dirty and covered with scratches.

The boys also had two garments, a hickory shirt and a pair of pants like their father's, made out of brown denims by the mother's never-resting hands—hands that in sleep still sewed, and skimmed, and baked, and churned. The boys had gone to bed without washing their feet, which now looked like toads, calloused, brown, and chapped.

Part of this the mother saw with her dull eyes as she came down, after seeing the departure of Sim up the road with the cows. It was a beautiful Sunday morning, and the woman might have sung like a bird if men had been as kind to her as Nature. But she looked dully out upon the seas of ripe grasses, tangled and flashing with dew, out of which the bobolinks and larks sprang. The glorious winds brought her no melody, no perfume, no respite from toil and care.

She thought of the children she saw in the town,—children of the merchant and banker, clean as little dolls, the boys in knickerbocker suits, the girls in dainty white dresses,—and a vengeful bitterness sprang up in her heart. She soon put the dishes away, but felt too tired and listless to do more.

"Taw-bay-wies! Pet want ta-aw-bay-wies!" cried the little one, tugging at her dress.

Listlessly, mechanically she took him in her arms, and went out into the garden, which was fragrant and sweet with dew and sun. After picking some berries for him, she sat down on the grass under the row of cottonwoods, and sank into a kind of lethargy. A kingbird chattered and shrieked overhead, the grasshoppers buzzed in the grasses, strange insects with ventriloquistic voices sang all about her—she could not tell where.

"Ma, can't I put on my clean dress?" insisted Sadie.

"I don't care," said the brooding woman, darkly. "Leave me alone."

Oh, if she could only lie here forever, escaping all pain and weariness! The wind sang in her ears; the great clouds, beautiful as heavenly ships, floated far above in the vast, dazzling deeps of blue sky; the birds rustled and chirped around her; leaping insects buzzed and clattered in the grass and in the vines and bushes. The goodness and glory of God was in the very air, the bitterness and oppression of man in every line of her face.

But her quiet was broken by Sadie, who came leaping like a fawn down through the grass.

"O ma, Aunt Maria and Uncle William are coming. They've jest turned in."

"I don't care if they be!" she answered in the same dully-irritated way. "What're they comin' here to-day for, I wan' to know." She stayed there immovably, till Mrs. Councill came down to see her, piloted by two or three of the children. Mrs. Councill, a jolly, large-framed woman, smiled brightly, and greeted her in a loud, jovial voice. She made the mistake of taking the whole matter lightly; her tone amounted to ridicule.

"Sim says you've been having a tantrum, Creeshy. Don't know what for, he says."

"He don't," said the wife, with a sullen flash in her eyes. "*He* don't know why! Well, then, you just tell him what I say. I've lived in hell long enough.

I'm done. I've slaved here day in and day out f'r twelve years without pay—not even a decent word. I've worked like no nigger ever worked 'r could work and live. I've given him all I had, 'r ever expect to have. I'm wore out. My strength is gone, my patience is gone. I'm done with it—that's a *part* of what's the matter."

"My sakes, Lucreeshy! You mustn't talk that way."

"But I *will*," said the woman, as she supported herself on one palm and raised the other. "I've *got* to talk that way." She was ripe for an explosion like this. She seized upon it with eagerness. "They ain't no use o' livin' this way, anyway. I'd take poison if it wa'n't f'r the young ones."

"Lucreeshy Burns!"

"Oh, I mean it."

"Land sakes alive, I b'lieve you're goin' crazy!"

"I shouldn't wonder if I was. I've had enough t' drive an Indian crazy. Now you jest go off an' leave me 'lone. I ain't no mind to visit—they ain't no way out of it, an' I'm tired o' tryin' to *find* a way. Go off an' let me be."

Her tone was so bitterly hopeless that the great, jolly face of Mrs. Councill stiffened into a look of horror such as she had not known for years. The children, in two separate groups, could be heard rioting. Bees were humming around the clover in the grass, and the kingbird chattered ceaselessly from the Lombardy poplar tip. Both women felt all this peace and beauty of the morning dimly, and it disturbed Mrs. Councill because the other was so impassive under it all. At last, after a long and thoughtful pause, Mrs. Councill asked a question whose answer she knew would decide it all—asked it very kindly and softly:

"Creeshy, are you comin' in?"

"No," was the short and sullenly decisive answer. Mrs. Councill knew that was the end, and so rose, with a sigh, and went away.

"Wal, good-by," she said, simply.

Looking back, she saw Lucretia lying at length, with closed eyes and hollow cheeks. She seemed to be sleeping, half-buried in the grass. She did not look up nor reply to her sister-in-law, whose life was one of toil and trouble, also, but not so hard and helpless as Lucretia's. By contrast with most of her neighbors, she seemed comfortable.

"Sim Burns, what you ben doin' to that woman?" she burst out, as she waddled up to where the two men were sitting under a cottonwood tree, talking and whittling after the manner of farmers.

"Nawthin' 's fur 's I know," answered Burns, not quite honestly, and looking uneasy.

"You needn't try t' git out of it like that, Sim Burns," replied his sister. "That woman never got into that fit f'r *nawthin'*."

"Wall, if you know more about it than I do, whadgy ask *me* fur?" he replied, angrily.

"Tut, tut!" put in Councill, "hold y'r horses! Don't git on y'r ear, children! Keep cool, and don't spile y'r shirts. Most likely you're all t' blame. Keep cool an' swear less."

"Wal, I'll bet Sim's more to blame than she is. Why, they ain't a harder-workin' woman in the hull State of Ioway than she is"——

"Except Marm Councill."

"Except nobody. Look at her, jest skin and bones."

Councill chuckled in his vast way. "That's so, mother; measured in that way, she leads over you. You git fat on it."

She smiled a little, her indignation oozing away. She never "*could* stay mad," her children were accustomed to tell her. Burns refused to talk any more about the matter, and the visitors gave it up, and got out their team and started for home, Mrs. Councill firing this parting shot:

"The best thing you can do to-day is t' let her alone. Mebbe the children 'll bring her round ag'in. If she does come round, you see 't you treat her a little more 's y' did when you was a-courtin' her."

"This way," roared Councill, putting his arm around his wife's waist. She boxed his ears, while he guffawed and clucked at his team.

Burns took a measure of salt and went out into the pasture to salt the cows. On the sunlit slope of the field, where the cattle came running and bawling to meet him, he threw down the salt in handfuls, and then lay down to watch them as they eagerly licked it up, even gnawing a bare spot in the sod in their eagerness to get it all.

Burns was not a drinking man; he was hard-working, frugal; in fact, he had no extravagances except his tobacco. His clothes he wore until they all but dropped from him; and he worked in rain and mud, as well as dust and sun. It was this suffering and toiling all to no purpose that made him sour and irritable. He didn't see why he should have so little after so much hard work.

He was puzzled to account for it all. His mind—the average mind—was weary with trying to solve an insoluble problem. His neighbors, who had got along a little better than himself, were free with advice and suggestion as to the cause of his persistent poverty.

Old man Bacon, the hardest-working man in the county, laid it to Burns's lack of management. Jim Butler, who owned a dozen farms (which he had taken on mortgages), and who had got rich by buying land at government price and holding for a rise, laid all such cases as Burns's to "lack of enterprise, foresight."

But the larger number, feeling themselves in the same boat with Burns, said:

"I d' know. Seems as if things get worse an' worse. Corn an' wheat gittin' cheaper 'n' cheaper. Machinery eatin' up profits—got to *have* machinery to harvest the cheap grain, an' then the machinery eats up profits. Taxes goin' up. Devil to pay all round; I d' know what in thunder *is* the matter."

The Democrats said protection was killing the farmers; the Republicans said no. The Grangers growled about the middle-men; the Greenbackers said there wasn't circulating medium enough, and, in the midst of it all, hard-working, discouraged farmers, like Simeon Burns, worked on, unable to find out what really was the matter.

And there, on this beautiful Sabbath morning, Sim sat and thought and thought, till he rose with an oath and gave it up.

IV.

IT was hot and brilliant again the next morning as Douglass Radbourn drove up the road with Lily Graham, the teacher of the school in the little white school-house. It was blazing hot, even though not yet nine o'clock, and the young farmers plowing beside the fence looked longingly and somewhat bitterly at Radbourn seated in a fine top-buggy beside a beautiful creature in lace and cambric.

Very beautiful the town-bred "school-ma'am" looked to those grimy, sweaty fellows, superb fellows, too, physically, with bare red arms and leather-colored faces. She was as if builded of the pink and white clouds soaring far up there in the morning sky. So cool, and sweet, and dainty.

As she came in sight, their dusty and sweaty shirts grew biting as the poisoned shirt of the Norse myth, their bare feet in the brown dirt grew distressingly flat and hoof-like, and their huge, dirty, brown, chapped and swollen hands grew so repulsive that the mere remote possibility of some time in the far future standing a chance of having an introduction to her caused them to wipe their palms on their trousers' legs stealthily.

Lycurgus Banks swore when he saw Radbourn. "That cuss thinks he's ol' hell this morning. He don't earn his living. But he's just the kind of cuss to get holt of all the purty girls."

Others gazed with simple, sad wistfulness upon the slender figure, pale, sweet face, and dark eyes of the young girl, feeling that to have talk with such a fairy-like creature was a happiness too great to ever be their lot. And when she had passed they went back to work with a sigh and feeling of loss.

As for Lily, she felt a pang of pity for these people. She looked at this peculiar form of poverty and hardship much as the fragile, tender girl of the city looks upon the men laying a gas-main in the streets. She felt, sympathetically, the heat and grime, and, though but the faintest idea of what it meant to wear such clothing came to her, she shuddered. Her eyes had been opened to these things by Radbourn, a class-mate at the Seminary.

The young fellow knew that Lily was in love with him, and he made distinct effort to keep the talk upon impersonal subjects. He liked her very much, probably because she listened so well.

"Poor fellows," sighed Lily, almost unconsciously. "I hate to see them working there in the dirt and hot sun. It seems a hopeless sort of life, doesn't it?"

"Oh, but this is the most beautiful part of the year," said Radbourn. "Think of them in the mud, in the sleet; think of them husking corn in the snow, a bitter wind blowing; think of them a month later in the harvest; think of them imprisoned here in winter!"

"Yes, it's dreadful! But I never felt it so keenly before. You have opened my eyes to it. Of course, I've been on a farm, but not to live there."

"Writers and orators have lied so long about 'the idyllic' in farm life, and said so much about the 'independent American farmer,' that he himself has remained blind to the fact that he's one of the hardest-working and poorest-paid men in America. See the houses they live in—hovels."

"Yes, yes, I know," said Lily; a look of deeper pain swept over her face. "And the fate of the poor women; oh, the fate of the women!"

"Yes, it's a matter of statistics," went on Radbourn, pitilessly, "that the wives of the American farmers fill our insane asylums. See what a life they lead, most of them; no music, no books. Seventeen hours a day in a couple of small rooms—dens. Now, there is Sim Burns! What a travesty of a home! Yet there are a dozen just as bad in sight. He works like a fiend—so does his wife—and what is their reward? Simply a hole to hibernate in and to sleep and eat in in summer. A dreary present and a well-nigh hopeless future. No, they have a future, if they knew it, and we must tell them."

"I know Mrs. Burns," Lily said, after a pause; "she sends several children to my school. Poor, pathetic little things, half-clad and wistful-eyed. They make my heart ache; they are so hungry for love, and so quick to learn."

As they passed the Burns farm, they looked for the wife, but she was not to be seen. The children had evidently gone up to the little white school-house at the head of the lane. Radbourn let the reins fall slack as he talked on. He did not look at the girl; his eyebrows were drawn into a look of gloomy pain.

"It ain't so much the grime that I abhor, nor the labor that crooks their backs and makes their hands bludgeons. It's the horrible waste of life involved in it all. I don't believe God intended a man to be bent to plow-handles like that, but that ain't the worst of it. The worst of it is, these people live lives approaching automata. They become machines to serve others more lucky or more unscrupulous than themselves. What is the world of art, of music, of literature, to these poor devils—to Sim Burns and his wife there, for example? Or even to the best of these farmers?"

The girl looked away over the shimmering lake of yellow-green corn. A choking came into her throat. Her gloved hand trembled.

"What is such a life worth? It's all very comfortable for us to say, 'They don't feel it.' How do we know what they feel? What do we know of their capacity for enjoyment of art and music? They never have leisure or opportunity. The master is very glad to be taught by preacher, and lawyer, and novelist, that his slaves are contented and never feel any longings for a higher life. These people live lives but little higher than their cattle—are *forced* to live so. Their hopes and aspirations are crushed out, their souls are twisted and deformed just as toil twists and deforms their bodies. They are on the same level as the city laborer. The very religion they hear is a soporific. They are taught to be content here that they may be happy hereafter. Suppose there isn't any hereafter?"

"Oh, don't say that, please!" Lily cried.

"But I don't *know* that there is," he went on remorselessly, "and I do know that these people are being robbed of something more than money, of all that makes life worth living. The promise of milk and honey in Canaan is all very well, but I prefer to have mine here; then I'm sure of it."

"What can we do?" murmured the girl.

"Do? Rouse these people for one thing; preach *discontent*, a noble discontent."

"It will only make them unhappy."

"No, it won't; not if you show them the way out. If it does, it's better to be unhappy striving for higher things, like a man, than to be content in a wallow like swine."

"But what *is* the way out?"

This was sufficient to set Radbourn upon his hobby-horse. He outlined his plan of action—the abolition of all indirect taxes; the State control of all privileges the private ownership of which interfered with the equal rights of all. He would utterly destroy speculative holdings of the earth. He would have land everywhere brought to its best use, by appropriating all ground rents to the use of the State, etc., etc., to which the girl listened with eager interest, but with only partial comprehension.

As they neared the little school-house, a swarm of midgets in pink dresses, pink sun-bonnets, and brown legs, came rushing to meet their teacher, with that peculiar devotion the children in the country develop for a refined teacher.

Radbourn helped Lily out into the midst of the eager little scholars, who swarmed upon her like bees on a lump of sugar, till even Radbourn's gravity gave way, and he smiled into her lifted eyes—an unusual smile, that strangely enough stopped the smile on her own lips, filling her face with a wistful shadow, and her breath came hard for a moment, and she trembled.

She loved that cold, stern face, oh, so much! and to have him smile was a pleasure that made her heart leap till she suffered a smothering pain. She turned to him to say:

"I am very thankful, Mr. Radbourn, for another pleasant ride," adding in a lower tone: "It was a very great pleasure; you always give me so much. I feel stronger and more hopeful."

"I'm glad you feel so. I was afraid I was prosy with my land-doctrine."

"Oh, no! Indeed no! You have given me a new hope; I am exalted with the thought; I shall try to think it all out and apply it."

And so they parted, the children looking on and slyly whispering among themselves. Radbourn looked back after awhile, but the bare little hive had absorbed its little group, and was standing bleak as a tombstone and hot as a furnace on the naked plain in the blazing sun.

"America's pitiful boast!" said the young radical, looking back at it. "Only a miserable hint of what it might be."

All that forenoon, as Lily faced her little group of barefooted children, she was thinking of Radbourn, of his almost fierce sympathy for these poor, supine farmers, hopeless and in some cases content in their narrow lives. The children almost worshiped the beautiful girl who came to them as a revelation of exquisite neatness and taste,—whose very voice and intonation awed them.

They noted, unconsciously, of course, every detail. Snowy linen, touches of soft color, graceful lines of bust and side—the slender fingers that could almost speak, so beautifully flexile were they. Lily herself sometimes, when she shook the calloused, knotted, stiffened hands of the women, shuddered with sympathetic pain, to think that the crowning wonder and beauty of God's world should be so maimed and distorted from its true purpose.

Even in the children before her she could see the inherited results of fruitless labor—and, more pitiful yet, in the bent shoulders of the older ones she could see the beginnings of deformity that would soon be permanent. And as these things came to her, she clasped the poor wondering things to her side with a convulsive wish to make life a little brighter for them.

"How is your mother to-day?" she asked of Sadie Burns, as she was eating her luncheon on the drab-colored table near the open window.

"Purty well," said Sadie, in a hesitating way.

Lily was looking out, and listening to the gophers whistling as they raced to and fro. She could see Bob Burns lying at length on the grass in the pasture over the fence, his heels waving in the air, his hands holding a string which formed a snare. It was like fishing to young Izaak Walton.

It was very still and hot, and the cheep and trill of the gophers and the chatter of the kingbirds alone broke the silence. A cloud of butterflies were fluttering about a pool near; a couple of big flies buzzed and mumbled on the pane.

"What ails your mother?" Lily asked, recovering herself and looking at Sadie, who was distinctly ill at ease.

"Oh, I dunno," Sadie replied, putting one bare foot across the other.

Lily insisted.

"She 'n' pa's had an awful row"——

"Sadie!" said the teacher warningly, "what language!"

"I mean they quarreled, an' she don't speak to him any more."

"Why, how dreadful!"

"An' pa he's awful cross; and she won't eat when he does, an' I haf to wait on table."

"I believe I'll go down and see her this noon," said Lily to herself, as she divined a little of the state of affairs in the Burns family.

V.

SIM was mending the pasture fence as Lily came down the road toward him. He had delayed going to dinner to finish his task and was just about ready to go when Lily spoke to him.

"Good morning, Mr. Burns. I am just going down to see Mrs. Burns. It must be time to go to dinner—aren't you ready to go? I want to talk with you."

Ordinarily he would have been delighted with the idea of walking down the road with the school-ma'am, but there was something in her look which seemed to tell him that she knew all about his trouble, and, besides, he was not in good humor.

"Yes, in a minnit—soon's I fix up this hole. Them shoats, I b'lieve, would go through a key-hole, if they could once get their snoots in."

He expanded on this idea as he nailed away, anxious to gain time. He foresaw trouble for himself. He couldn't be rude to this sweet and fragile girl. If a *man* had dared to attack him on his domestic shortcomings, he could have fought. The girl stood waiting for him, her large, steady eyes full of thought, gazing down at him from the shadow of her broad-brimmed hat.

"The world is so full of misery anyway, that we ought to do the best we can to make it less," she said at last, in a musing tone, as if her thoughts had unconsciously taken on speech. She had always appealed to him strongly, and never more so than in this softly-uttered abstraction—that it was an abstraction added to its power with him.

He could find no words for reply, but picked up his hammer and nail-box, and slouched along the road by her side, listening without a word to her talk.

"Christ was patient, and bore with his enemies. Surely we ought to bear with our—friends," she went on, adapting her steps to his. He took off his torn straw hat and wiped his face on his sleeve, being much embarrassed and ashamed. Not knowing how to meet such argument, he kept silent.

"How *is* Mrs. Burns?" said Lily at length, determined to make him speak. The delicate meaning in the emphasis laid on *is* did not escape him.

"Oh, she's all right—I mean she's done her work jest the same as ever. I don't see her much"——

"I didn't know—I was afraid she was sick. Sadie said she was acting strangely."

"No, she's well enough—but"——

"But what is the trouble? Won't you let me help you, *won't* you?" she pleaded.

"Can't anybody help us. We've got 'o fight it out, I s'pose," he replied, a gloomy note of resentment creeping into his voice. "She's ben in a devil of a temper f'r a week."

"Haven't you been in the same kind of a temper too?" demanded Lily, firmly, but kindly. "I think most troubles of this kind come from bad temper on both sides. Don't you? Have you done your share at being kind and patient?"

They had reached the gate now, and she laid her hand on his arm to stop him. He looked down at the slender gloved hand on his arm, feeling as if a giant had grasped him; then he raised his eyes to her face, flushing a purplish red as he remembered his grossness. It seemed monstrous in the presence of this girl-advocate. Her face was like silver; her eyes seemed pools of tears.

"I don't s'pose I have," he said at last, pushing by her. He could not have faced her glance another moment. His whole air conveyed the impression of destructive admission. Lily did not comprehend the extent of her advantage or she would have pursued it further. As it was she felt a little hurt as she entered the house. The table was set, but Mrs. Burns was nowhere to be seen. Calling her softly, the young girl passed through the shabby little living-room to the oven-like bed-room which opened off it, but no one was about. She stood for a moment shuddering at the wretchedness of the room.

Going back to the kitchen, she found Sim about beginning on his dinner. Little Pet was with him; the rest of the children were at the school-house.

"Where is she?"

"I d' know. Out in the garden, I expect. She don't eat with me now. I never see her. She don't come near *me*. I ain't seen her since Saturday."

Lily was shocked inexpressibly and began to see more clearly the magnitude of the task she had set herself to do. But it must be done; she felt that a tragedy was not far off. It must be averted.

"Mr. Burns, what have you done? What *have* you done?" she asked in terror and horror.

"Don't lay it all to *me*! She hain't done nawthin' but complain f'r ten years. I couldn't do nothin' to suit her. She was always naggin' me."

"I don't think Lucretia Burns would nag anybody. I don't say you're *all* to blame, but I'm afraid you haven't acknowledged you were *any* to blame. I'm afraid you've not been patient with her. I'm going out to bring her in. If she comes, will you *say* you were *part* to blame? You needn't beg her pardon— just say you'll try to be better. Will you do it? Think how much she has done for you! Will you?"

He remained silent, and looked discouragingly rude. His sweaty, dirty shirt was open at the neck, his arms were bare, his scraggly teeth were yellow with tobacco, and his uncombed hair lay tumbled about on his high, narrow head. His clumsy, unsteady hands played with the dishes on the table. His pride was struggling with his sense of justice; he knew he ought to consent, and yet it was so hard to acknowledge himself to blame. The girl went on in a voice piercingly sweet, trembling with pity and pleading.

"What word can I carry to her from you? I'm going to go and see her. If I could take a word from *you*, I know she would come back to the table. Shall I tell her you feel to blame?"

The answer was a long time coming; at last the man nodded an assent, the sweat pouring from his purple face. She had set him thinking; her victory was sure.

Lily almost ran out into the garden and to the strawberry patch, where she found Lucretia in her familiar, colorless, shapeless dress, picking berries in the hot sun, the mosquitoes biting her neck and hands.

"Poor, pathetic, dumb sufferer!" the girl thought as she ran up to her.

She dropped her dish as she heard Lily coming, and gazed up into the tender, pitying face. Not a word was spoken, but something she saw there made her eyes fill with tears, and her throat swell. It was pure sympathy. She put her arms around the girl's neck and sobbed for the first time since Friday night. Then they sat down on the grass under the hedge, and she told her story, interspersed with Lily's horrified comments.

When it was all told, the girl still sat listening. She heard Radbourn's calm, slow voice again. It helped her not to hate Burns; it helped her to pity and understand him:

"You must remember that such toil brutalizes a man; it makes him callous, selfish, unfeeling, necessarily. A fine nature must either adapt itself to its hard surroundings or die. Men who toil terribly in filthy garments day after day and year after year cannot easily keep gentle; the frost and grime, the heat and cold will soon or late enter into their souls. The case is not all in favor of the suffering wives, and against the brutal husbands. If the farmer's wife is dulled and crazed by her routine, the farmer himself is degraded and brutalized."

As well as she could Lily explained all this to the woman, who lay with her face buried in the girl's lap. Lily's arms were about her thin shoulders in an agony of pity.

"It's hard, Lucretia, I know—more than you can bear—but you mustn't forget what Sim endures too. He goes out in the storms and in the heat and dust. His boots are hard, and see how his hands are all bruised and broken by his work! He was tired and hungry when he said that—he didn't really mean it."

The wife remained silent.

"Mr. Radbourn says work, as things go now, *does* degrade a man in spite of himself. He says men get coarse and violent in spite of themselves, just as women do when everything goes wrong in the house—when the flies are thick, and the fire won't burn, and the irons stick to the clothes. You see, you both suffer. Don't lay up this fit of temper against Sim—will you?"

The wife lifted her head and looked away. Her face was full of hopeless weariness.

"It ain't this once. It ain't that 't all. It's having no let-up. Just goin' the same thing right over 'n' over—no hope of anything better."

"If you had a hope of another world"——

"Don't talk that. I don't want that kind o' comfort. I want a decent chance here. I want 'o rest an' be happy *now*." Lily's big eyes were streaming with tears. What should she say to the desperate woman? "What's the use? We might jest as well die—all of us."

The woman's livid face appalled the girl. She was gaunt, heavy-eyed, nerveless. Her faded dress settled down over her limbs, showing the swollen knees and thin calves; her hands, with distorted joints, protruded painfully from her sleeves. And all about was the ever-recurring wealth and cheer of nature that knows no fear or favor—the bees and flies buzzing in the sun, the jay and kingbird in the poplars, the smell of strawberries, the motion of lush grass, the shimmer of corn-blades tossed gayly as banners in a conquering army.

Like a flash of keener light, a sentence shot across the girl's mind: "Nature knows no title-deed. The bounty of her mighty hands falls as the sunlight falls, copious, impartial; her seas carry all ships; her air is for all lips, her lands for all feet."

"Poverty and suffering such as yours will not last." There was something in the girl's voice that roused the woman. She turned her dull eyes upon the youthful face.

Lily took her hand in both hers as if by a caress she could impart her own faith.

"Look up, dear. When nature is so good and generous, man must come to be better, surely. Come, go in the house again. Sim is there; he expects you; he told me to tell you he was sorry." Lucretia's face twitched a little at that, but her head was bent. "Come; you can't live this way. There isn't any other place to go to."

No; that was the bitterest truth. Where on this wide earth, with its forth-shooting fruits and grains, its fragrant lands and shining seas, could this dwarfed, bent, broken, middle-aged woman go? Nobody wanted her, nobody cared for her. But the wind kissed her drawn lips as readily as those of the girl, and the blooms of clover nodded to her as if to a queen.

Lily had said all she could. Her heart ached with unspeakable pity and a sort of terror.

"Don't give up, Lucretia. This may be the worst hour of your life. Live and bear with it all for Christ's sake—for your children's sake. Sim told me to tell you he was to blame. If you will only see that you are both to blame and yet neither to blame, then you can rise above it. Try, dear!"

Something that was in the girl imparted itself to the wife, electrically. She pulled herself together, rose silently, and started toward the house. Her face was rigid, but no longer sullen. Lily followed her slowly, wonderingly.

As she neared the kitchen door, she saw Sim still sitting at the table; his face was unusually grave and soft. She saw him start and shove back his chair—saw Lucretia go to the stove and lift the tea-pot, and heard her say, as she took her seat beside the baby:

"Want some more tea?"

She had become a wife and mother again, but in what spirit the puzzled girl could not say.

Part V.

SATURDAY NIGHT ON THE FARM BOYS AND HARVEST HANDS.

In mystery of town and play
The splendid lady lives alway,
Inwrought with starlight, winds and streams.

SATURDAY NIGHT ON THE FARM.

A GROUP of men were gathered in Farmer Graham's barn one rainy day in September; the rain had stopped the stacking, and the men were amusing themselves with feats of skill and strength. Steve Nagle was the champion, no matter what came up; whether shouldering a sack of wheat, or raising weights or suspending himself with one hand, he left the others out of the race.

"Aw! it's no good foolun' with such puny little men as you," he swaggered at last, throwing himself down upon a pile of sacks.

"If our hired man was here I bet he'd beat you all holler," piped a boy's voice from the doorway.

Steve raised himself up and glared.

"What's that thing talkun'?"

The boy held his ground. "You can brag when he ain't around, but I bet he can lick you with one hand tied behind him; don't you, Frank?"

Frank was doubtful, and kept a little out of sight. He was afraid of Steve, as were, indeed, all the other men, for he had terrorized the saloons of the county for years. Johnny went on about his hero:

"Why, he can take a sack of wheat by the corners and snap every kernel of it clean out; he can lift a separator just as easy! You'd better brag when he's around."

Steve's anger rose, for he saw the rest laughing; he glared around at them all like a hyena. "Bring on this whelp, let's see how he looks. I ain't seen him yit."

"Pa says if Lime went to a saloon where you'd meet him once, you wouldn't clean out that saloon," Johnny went on in a calm voice, with a sort of undercurrent of glee in it. He saw Steve's anger, and was delighted.

"Bring on this feller; I'll knock the everlasting spots offen 'im f'r two cents."

"I'll tell 'im that."

"Tell him and be damned," roared Steve, with a wolfish gleam in his eyes that drove the boys away whooping with mingled terror and delight.

Steve saw that the men about him held Johnny's opinion of Lime, and it made him furious. For several years he had held undisputed sovereignty over the saloons of Rock County, and when, with both sleeves rolled up and eyes flaming with madness, he had leaped into the center of a bar-room floor with a wild shout, everybody got out, by doors, windows or any other way, sometimes taking sash and all, and left him roaring with maniacal delight.

No one used a revolver in those days. Shooting was almost unknown. Fights were tests of physical strength and savagery.

Harvest brought into Iowa at that time a flood of rough and hardy men who drifted north with the moving line of ripening wheat, and on Saturday nights the saloons of the county were filled with them, and Steve found many chances to show his power. Among these strangers, as they gathered in some saloon to make a night of it, he loved to burst with his assertion of individual sovereignty.

Lime was out mending fence when Johnny came home to tell him what Steve had said. Johnny was anxious to see his faith in his hero justified, and watched Lime carefully as he pounded away without looking up. His dress always had an easy slouch about his vast limbs, and his pantaloons, usually of some dark stuff, he wore invariably tucked into his boot-tops, his vest swinging unbuttoned, his hat carelessly awry.

Being a quiet, sober man, he had never been in a saloon when Steve entered to swing his hat to the floor and yell:

"I'm Jack Robinson, I am! I am the man that bunted the bull off the bridge! I'm the best man in Northern Iowa!" He had met him, of course, but Steve kept a check upon himself when sober.

"He says he can knock the spots off of you," Johnny said, in conclusion, watching Lime roguishly.

The giant finished nailing up the fence, and at last said: "Now run along, sonny, and git the cows." There was a laugh in his voice that showed his amusement at Johnny's disappointment. "I ain't got any spots."

On the following Saturday night, at dusk, as Lime was smoking his pipe out on the horse-block, with the boys around him, there came a swiftly-driven wagon down the road, filled with a noisy load of men. They pulled up at the gate, with a prodigious shouting.

"Hello, Lime!"

"Hello, the house!"

"Hurrah for the show!"

"It's Al Crandall," cried Johnny, running down to the gate. Lime followed slowly, and asked: "What's up, boys?"

"All goin' down to the show; climb in!"

"All right; wait till I git my coat."

Lime was working one of Graham's farms on shares in the summer; in the winter he went to the pinery.

"Oh, can't we go, Lime?" pleaded the boys.

"If your dad'll let you; I'll pay for the tickets."

The boys rushed wildly to the house and as wildly back again, and the team resumed its swift course, for it was getting late. It was a beautiful night; the full moon poured down a cataract of silent white light like spray, and the dew (almost frost) lay on the grass and reflected the glory of the autumn sky; the air was still and had that peculiar property, common to the prairie air, of carrying sound to a great distance.

The road was hard and smooth, and the spirited little team bowled the heavy wagon along at a swift pace. "We're late," Crandall said, as he snapped his long whip over the heads of his horses, "and we've got to make it in twenty-five minutes or miss part of the show." This caused Johnny great anxiety. He had never seen a play and wanted to see it all. He looked at the flying legs of the horses and pushed on the dashboard, chirping at them slyly.

Rock Falls was the county town and the only town where plays could be produced. It was a place of about 3,000 inhabitants at that time, and to Johnny's childish eyes it was a very great place indeed. To go to town was an event, but to go with the men at night, and to a show, was something to remember a lifetime.

There was little talk as they rushed along, only some singing of a dubious sort by Bill Young, on the back seat. At intervals Bill stopped singing and leaned over to say, in exactly the same tone of voice each time: "Al, I hope t' God we won't be late." Then he resumed his monotonous singing, or said something coarse to Rice, who laughed immoderately.

The play had begun when they climbed the narrow, precarious stairway which led to the door of the hall. Every seat of the room was filled, but as for the boys, after getting their eyes upon the players, they did not think of sitting, or of moving, for that matter; they were literally all eyes and ears.

The hall seated about 400 persons, and the stage was a contrivance striking as to coloring as well as variety of pieces. It added no little to the sport of the evening by the squeaks it gave out as the heavy man walked across, and by the falling down of the calico wings and by the persistent refusal of the curtain to go down at the proper moment on the tableau. At the back of the room the benches rose one above the other until the one at the rear was near the grimy ceiling. These benches were occupied by the toughs of the town, who treated each other to peanuts and slapped one another over the head with their soft, shapeless hats, and laughed inordinately when some fellow's hat was thrown out of his reach into the crowd.

The play was Wilkie Collins' "New Magdalen," and the part of Mercy was taken by a large and magnificently proportioned woman, a blonde, and in Johnny's eyes she seemed something divine, with her grace and majesty of motion. He took a personal pride in her at once and wanted her to come out triumphant in the end, regardless of any conventional morality.

True, his admiration for the dark little woman's tragic utterance at times drew him away from his breathless study of the queenly Mercy, but such moments were few. Within a half hour he was deeply in love with the heroine and wondered how she could possibly endure the fat man who played the part of Horace, and who pitched into the practicable supper of cold ham, biscuit and currant wine with a gusto that suggested gluttony as the reason for his growing burden of flesh.

And so the play went on. The wonderful old lady in the cap and spectacles, the mysterious dark little woman who popped in at short intervals to say "Beware!" in a very deep contralto voice, the tender and repentant Mercy, all were new and wonderful, beautiful things to the boys, and though they stood up the whole evening through, it passed so swiftly that the curtain's fall drew from them long sighs of regret. From that time on they were to dream of that wonderful play and that beautiful, repentant woman. So securely was she enthroned in their regard that no rude and senseless jest could ever unseat her. Of course, the men, as they went out, laughed and joked in the manner of such men, and swore in their disappointment because it was a serious drama in place of the comedy and the farce which they had expected.

"It's a regular sell," Bill said. "I wanted to hear old Plunket stid of all that stuff about nothin'. That was a lunkin' good-lookin' woman though," he added, with a coarse suggestion in his voice, which exasperated Johnny to the pitch of giving him a kick on the heel as he walked in front. "Hyare, young feller, look where you're puttin' your hoofs!" Bill growled, looking about.

John was comforted by seeing in the face of his brother the same rapt expression which he felt was on his own. He walked along almost mechanically, scarcely feeling the sidewalk, his thoughts still dwelling on the lady and the play. It was after ten o'clock, and the stores were all shut, the frost lay thick and white on the plank walk, and the moon was shining as only a moon can shine through the rarefied air on the Western prairies, and overhead the stars in innumerable hosts swam in the absolutely cloudless sky.

John stumbled along, keeping hold of Lime's hand till they reached the team standing at the sidewalk, shivering with cold. The impatient horses stretched their stiffened limbs with pleasure and made off with a rearing plunge. The men were noisy. Bill sang another song at the top of his voice as they rattled by the sleeping houses, but as he came to an objectionable part of the song Lime turned suddenly and said: "Shut up on that, will you?" and he became silent.

Rock Falls, after the most extraordinary agitation, had just prohibited the sale of liquor at any point within two miles of the school-house in the town. This, after strenuous opposition, was enforced; the immediate effect of the law was to establish saloons at the limit of the two miles and to throw a large increase of business into the hands of Hank Swartz in the retail part of his brewery, which was situated about two miles from the town, on the bank of the river. He had immediately built a bar-room and made himself ready for the increase of his trade, which had previously been confined to supplying picnic parties with half-kegs of beer or an occasional glass to teamsters passing by. Hank had an eye to the main chance and boasted: "If the public gits ahead of me it's got to be up and a-comin'."

The road along which Crandall was driving did not lead to Hank's place, but the river road, which branched off a little farther on, went by the brewery, though it was a longer way around. The men grew silent at last, and the steady roll and rumble of the wagon over the smooth road was soothing, and John laid his head in Lime's lap and fell asleep while looking at the moon and wondering why it always seemed to go just as fast as the team.

He was awakened by a series of wild yells, the snapping of whips and the furious rush of horses. It was another team filled with harvesters trying to pass, and not succeeding. The fellows in the other wagon hooted and howled and cracked the whip, but Al's little bays kept them behind until Lime protested, "Oh, let 'em go, Al," and then with a shout of glee the team went by and left them in a cloud of dust.

"Say, boys," said Bill, "that was Pat Sheehan and the Nagle boys. They've turned off; they're goin' down to Hank's. Let's go too. Come on, fellers, what d'you say? I'm allfired dry. Ain't you?"

"I'm willun'," said Frank Rice; "what d'you say, Lime?" John looked up into Lime's face and said to him, in a low voice, "Let's go home; that was Steve a-drivin'." Lime nodded and made a sign to John to keep still, but John saw his head lift. He had heard and recognized Steve's voice.

"It was Pat Sheehan, sure," repeated Bill, "an' I shouldn't wonder if the others was the Nagle boys and Eth Cole."

"Yes, it was Steve," said Al. "I saw his old hat as he went by."

It was perfectly intelligible to Lime that they were all anxious to have a meeting between Steve and himself. Johnny saw also that if Lime refused to go to the brewery he would be called a coward. Bill would tell it all over the neighborhood, and his hero would be shamed. At last Lime nodded his head in consent and Al turned off into the river road.

When they drew up at the brewery by the river the other fellows had all entered and the door was shut. There were two or three other teams hitched about under the trees. The men sprang out and Bill danced a jig in anticipation of the fun to follow. "If Steve starts to lam Lime there'll be a circus."

As they stood for a moment before the door Al spoke to Lime about Steve's probable attack. "I ain't goin' to hunt around for no row," replied Lime, placidly, "and I don't believe Steve is. You lads," he said to the boys, "watch the team for a little while; cuddle down under the blankets if you git cold. It ain't no place for you in the inside. We won't stop long," he ended, cheerily.

The door opened and let out a dull red light, closed again, and all was still except an occasional burst of laughter and noise of heavy feet within. The scene made an indelible impress upon John, child though he was. Fifty feet away the river sang over its shallows, broad and whitened with foam which gleamed like frosted silver in the brilliant moonlight. The trees were dark and tall about him and loomed overhead against the starlit sky, and the broad high moon threw a thick tracery of shadows on the dusty white road where the horses stood. Only the rhythmic flow of the broad, swift river, with the occasional uneasy movement of the horses under their creaking harnesses or the dull noise of the shouting men within the shanty, was to be heard.

John nestled down into the robes and took to dreaming of the lovely lady he had seen, and wondered if, when he became a man, he should have a wife like her. He was awakened by Frank, who was rousing him to serve a purpose of his own. John was ten and Frank fifteen; he rubbed his sleepy eyes and rose under orders.

"Say, Johnny, what d'yeh s'pose them fellers are doen' in there? You said Steve was goin' to lick Lime, you did. It don't sound much like it in there. Hear 'um laugh," he said viciously and regretfully. "Say, John, you sly along and peek in and see what they're up to, an' come an' tell me, while I hold the horses," he said, to hide the fact that John was doing a good deal for his benefit.

John got slowly off the wagon and hobbled on toward the saloon, stiff with the cold. As he neared the door he could hear some one talking in a loud voice, while the rest laughed at intervals in the manner of those who are listening to the good points in a story. Not daring to open the door, Johnny stood around the front trying to find a crevice to look in at. The speaker inside had finished his joke and some one had begun singing.

The building was a lean-to attached to the brewery, and was a rude and hastily constructed affair. It had only two windows; one was on the side and the other on the back. The window on the side was out of John's reach, so he went to the back of the shanty. It was built partly into the hill, and the window was at the top of the bank. John found that by lying down on the ground on the outside he had a good view of the interior. The window, while level with the ground on the outside, was about as high as the face of a man on the inside. He was extremely wide-awake now and peered in at the scene with round, unblinking eyes.

Steve was making sport for the rest and stood leaning his elbow on the bar. He was in rare good humor, for him. His hat was lying beside him and he was in his shirt-sleeves, and his cruel gray eyes, pockmarked face and broken nose were lighted up with a frightful smile. He was good-natured now, but the next drink might set him wild. Hank stood behind the high pine bar, a broad but nervous grin on his round, red face. Two big kerosene lamps, through a couple of smoky chimneys, sent a dull red glare upon the company, which half filled the room.

If Steve's face was unpleasant to look upon, the nonchalant, tiger-like poise and flex of his body was not. He had been dancing, it seemed, and had thrown off his coat, and as he talked he repeatedly rolled his blue shirt-sleeves up and down as though the motion were habitual to him. Most of the men were sitting around the room looking on and laughing at Steve's antics, and the antics of one or two others who were just drunk enough to make fools of themselves. Two or three sat on an old billiard table under the window through which John was peering.

Lime sat in his characteristic attitude, his elbows upon his knees and his thumbs under his chin. His eyes were lazily raised now and then with a lion-like action of the muscles of his forehead. But he seemed to take little interest in the ribaldry of the other fellows. John measured both champions critically, and exulted in the feeling that Steve was not so ready for the row with Lime as he thought he was.

After Steve had finished his story there was a chorus of roars: "Bully for you, Steve!" "Give us another," etc. Steve, much flattered, nodded to the alert saloon-keeper, and said: "Give us another, Hank." As the rest all sprang up he added: "Pull out that brandy kaig this time, Hank. Trot her out, you white-livered Dutchman," he roared, as Swartz hesitated.

The brewer fetched it up from beneath the bar, but he did it reluctantly. In the midst of the hubbub thus produced, an abnormally tall and lanky fellow known as "High" Bedloe pushed up to the bar and made an effort to speak, and finally did say solemnly:

"Gen'lmun, Steve, say, gen'lmun, do'n' less mix our drinks!"

This was received with boisterous delight, in which Bedloe could not see the joke, and looked feebly astonished.

Just at this point John received such a fright as entirely took away his powers of moving or breathing, for something laid hold of his heels with deadly grip. He was getting his breath to yell when a familiar voice at his ear said, in a tone somewhere between a whisper and a groan:

"Say, what they up to all this while? I'm sick o' wait'n' out there."

Frank had become impatient; as for John, he had been so absorbed by the scenes within, he had not noticed how the frosty ground was slowly stiffening his limbs and setting his teeth chattering. They were both now looking in at the window. John had simply pointed with his mittened, stubby thumb toward the interior, and Frank had crawled along to a place beside him.

Mixing the drinks had produced the disastrous effect which Hank and Bedloe had anticipated. The fun became uproarious. There were songs and dances by various members of the Nagle gang, but Lime's crowd, being in the minority, kept quiet, occasionally standing treat as was the proper thing to do.

But Steve grew wilder and more irritable every moment. He seemed to have drunk just enough to let loose the terrible force that slept in his muscles. He had tugged at his throat until the strings of his woolen shirt loosened, displaying the great, sloping muscles of his neck and shoulders, white as milk and hard as iron. His eyes rolled restlessly to and fro as he paced the floor. His panther-like step was full of a terrible suggestiveness. The breath of the boys at the window came quicker and quicker. They saw he was working himself into a rage that threatened momentarily to break forth into a violence. He realized that this was a crisis in his career; his reputation was at stake.

Young as John was, he understood the whole matter as he studied the restless Steve, and compared him with his impassive hero, sitting immovable.

"You see Lime can't go away," he explained, breathlessly, to Frank, in a whisper, "'cause they'd tell it all over the country that he backed down for Steve. He daresn't leave."

"Steve ain't no durn fool," returned the superior wisdom of Frank, in the same cautious whisper, keeping his eyes on the bar-room. "See Lime there, cool as a cucumber. He's from the pineries, he is." He ended in a tone of voice intended to convey that fighting was the principal study of the pineries, and that Lime had graduated with the highest honors. "Steve ain't a-go'n' to pitch into him yet awhile, you bet y'r bottom dollar; he ain't drunk enough for that."

Each time the invitation for another drink was given, they noticed that Lime kept on the outside of the crowd, and some one helped him to his glass. "Don't you see he ain't drinkin'. He's throwin' it away," said Frank; "there, see! He's foolun' 'em; he ain't a-go'n' to be drunk when Steve tackles him. Oh, there'll be music in a minute or two."

Steve now walked the floor, pouring forth a flood of profanity and challenges against men who were not present. He had not brought himself to the point of attacking the unmoved and silent giant. Some of the younger men, and especially the pleader against mixed drinks, had succumbed, and were sleeping heavily on the back end of the bar and on the billiard table. Hank was getting anxious, and the forced smile on his face was painful to see. Over the whole group there was a singular air of waiting. No one was enjoying himself, and all wished that they were on the road home, but there was no way out of it now. It was evident that Lime purposed forcing the beginning of the battle on Steve. He sat in statuesque repose.

Steve had got his hat in his hand and held it doubled up like a club, and every time that he turned in his restless walk he struck the bar a resounding blow. His eyes seemed to see nothing, although they moved wildly from side to side.

He lifted up his voice in a raucous snarl. "I'm the man that struck Billy Patterson! I'm the man that bunted the bull off the bridge! Anybody got anything to say, now's his time. I'm here. Bring on your champion."

Foam came into the corners of his mouth, and the veins stood out on his neck. His red face shone with its swollen veins. He smashed his fists together, threw his hat on the floor, tramped on it, snarling out curses. Nothing kept him in check save the imperturbability of the seated figure. Everybody expected him to clear the saloon to prove his power.

Bedloe, who was asleep on the table, precipitated matters by rolling off with a prodigious noise amid a pandemonium of howls and laughter. In his anxiety to see what was going on, Frank thrust his head violently against the window, and it crashed in, sending the glass rattling down on the table.

Steve looked up, a red sheen in his eyes like that of a wild beast. Instantly his fury burst out against this new object of attention—a wild, unreasoning rage.

"What you doen' there? Who air ye, ye mangy little dog?"

Both boys sank back in tumultuous, shuddering haste, and rolled down the embankment, while they heard the voice of Steve thundering: "Fetch the little whelp here!"

There was a rush from the inside, a sudden outpouring, and the next moment John felt a hand touch his shoulder. Steve dragged him around to the front of the saloon before he could draw his breath or utter a sound. The rest crowded around.

"What are y' doen' there?" said Steve, shaking him with insane vindictiveness.

"Drop that boy!" said the voice of Lime, and voice never sounded sweeter. "Drop that boy!" he repeated, and his voice had a peculiar sound, as if it came through his teeth.

Steve dropped him, and turned with a grating snarl upon Lime, who opened his way through the excited crowd while Johnny stumbled, leaped and crawled out of the ring and joined Frank.

"Oh, it's you, is it? You white-livered"——He did not finish, for the arm of the blond giant shot out against his face like a beetle, and down he rolled on the grass. The sound of the blow made Johnny give an involuntary, quick cry.

"No human bein' could have stood up agin that blow," Crandall said afterwards. "It was like a mule a-kickin'."

As Steve slowly gained his feet, the silence was so great that Johnny could hear the thumping of his heart and the fierce, almost articulate breathing of Steve. The chatter and roar of the drunken crowd had been silenced by this encounter of the giants. The open door, where Hank stood, sent a reddish bar of light upon the two men as they faced each other with a sort of terrific calm. In his swift gaze in search of his brother, John noticed the dark wood, the river murmuring drowsily over its foam-wreathed pebbles, and saw his brother's face white with excitement, but not fear.

Lime's blow had dazed Steve for a moment, but at the same time it had sobered him. He came to his feet with a rising mutter that sounded like the swelling snarl of a tiger. He had been taken by surprise before, and he now came forward with his hands in position, to vindicate his terrible reputation. The two men met in a frightful struggle. Blows that meant murder were dealt by each. Each slapping thud seemed to carry the cracking of bones in it. Steve was the more agile of the two and circled rapidly around, striking like a boxer.

Every time his face came into view, with set teeth and ferocious scowl, the boys' spirits fell. But when they saw the calm, determined eyes of Lime, his watchful, confident look, they grew assured. All depended upon him. The Nagle gang were like wolves in their growing ferocity, and as they outnumbered the other party two to one, it was a critical quarter of an hour. In a swift retrospect they remembered the frightful tales told of this very spot—of the killing of Lars Peterson and his brother Nels, and the brutal hammering a crowd of drunken men had given to Big Ole, of the Wapsy.

The blood was trickling down Lime's face from a cut on his cheek, but Steve's face was swollen and ghastly from the three blows which he had received. Lime was saving himself for a supreme effort. The Nagle party, encouraged by the sound of the blows which Steve struck, began to yell and to show that they were ready to take a hand in the contest.

"Go it, Steve, we'll back yeh! Give it to 'im. We're with yeh! We'll tend to the rest." They began to pull off their coats.

Rice also threw off his coat. "Never mind these cowards, Lime. Hold on! Fair play!" he yelled, as he saw young Nagle about to strike Lime from behind.

His cry startled Lime, and with a sudden leap he dealt Steve a terrible blow full in the face, and as he went reeling back made another leaping lunge and struck him to the ground—a motion that seemed impossible to one of his bulk. But as he did so one of the crowd tripped him and sent him rolling upon the prostrate Steve, whose friends leaped like a pack of snarling wolves upon Lime's back. There came into the giant's heart a terrible, blind, desperate resolution. With a hoarse, inarticulate cry he gathered himself for one supreme effort and rose from the heap like a bear shaking off a pack of dogs; and holding the stunned and nerveless Steve in his great hands, with one swift, incredible effort literally swept his opponent's body in the faces of the infuriated men rushing down upon him.

"Come on, you red hellions!" he shouted, in a voice like a lion at bay. The light streamed on his bared head, his hands were clinched, his chest heaved in great gasps. There was no movement. The crowd waited with their hands lowered; before such a man they could not stand for a moment. They could not meet the blaze of his eyes. For a moment it seemed as if no one breathed.

In the silence that followed, Bill, who had kept out of sight up to this moment, piped out in a high, weak falsetto, with a comically questioning accent: "All quiet along the Potomac, boys?"

Lime unbraced, wiped his face and laughed. The others joined in cautiously. "No, thank yez, none in mine," said Sheehan, in answer to the challenge of Lime. "Whan Oi take to fightin' stame-ingins Oi'll lit you knaw."

"Well, I should say so," said another. "Lime, you're the best man that walks this State."

"Git out of the way, you white-livered hound, or I'll blow hell out o' yeh," said Steve, who had recovered himself sufficiently to know what it all meant. He lay upon the grass behind the rest and was weakly trying to get his revolver sighted upon Lime. One of the men caught him by the shoulder and the rest yelled:

"Hyare, Steve, no shootin'. It was a fair go, and you're whipped."

Steve only repeated his warnings to get out of the way. Lime turned upon him and kicked the weapon from his outstretched hand, breaking his arm at the wrist. The bullet went flying harmlessly into the air, and the revolver hurtled away into the shadows.

Walking through the ring, Lime took John by the hand and said: "Come, boy, this is no place for you. Let's go home. Fellers," he drawled in his customary lazy way, "when y' want me you know where to find me. Come, boys, the circus is over, the last dog is hung."

For the first mile or two there was a good deal of talk, and Bill said he knew that Lime could whip the whole crowd.

"But where was you, Bill, about the time they had me down? I don't remember hearin' anything of you 'long about that time, Bill."

Bill had nothing to say.

"Made me think somehow of Daniel in the lions' den," said Johnny.

"What do you mean by that, Johnny?" said Bill. "It made me think of a circus. The circus there'll be when Lime's woman finds out what he's been a-doin'."

"Great Scott, boys, you mustn't tell on me," said Lime, in genuine alarm.

As for John, he lay with his head in Lime's lap, looking up at the glory of the starlit night, and with a confused mingling of the play, of the voice of the lovely woman, of the shouts and blows at the brewery in his mind, and with the murmur of the river and the roll and rumble of the wagon blending in his ears, he fell into a sleep which the rhythmic beat of the horses' hoofs did not interrupt.

Part VI.

VILLAGE CRONIES
A GAME OF CHECKERS AT THE GROCERY.

The village life abounds with jokers,
Shiftless, conscienceless and shrewd.

SOME VILLAGE CRONIES.

COLONEL PEAVY had just begun the rubber with Squire Gordon, of Cerro Gordo County. They were seated in Robie's grocery, behind the rusty old cannon stove, the checker-board spread out on their knees. The Colonel was grinning in great glee, wringing his bony yellow hands in nervous excitement, in strong contrast to the stolid calm of the fat Squire.

The Colonel had won the last game by a large margin, and was sure he had his opponent's dodges well in hand. It was early in the evening, and the grocery was comparatively empty. Robie was figuring at a desk, and old Judge Brown stood in legal gravity warming his legs at the red-hot stove, and swaying gently back and forth in speechless content. It was a tough night outside, one of the toughest for years. The frost had completely shut the window panes as with thick blankets of snow. The streets were silent.

"I don't know," said the Judge, reflectively, to Robie, breaking the silence in his rasping, judicial bass, "I don't know as there has been such a night as this since the night of February 2d, '59; that was the night James Kirk went under—Honorable Kirk, you remember—knew him well. Brilliant fellow, ornament to Western bar. But whisky downed him. It'll beat the oldest man—I wonder where the boys all are to-night? Don't seem to be any one stirring on the street. Ain't frightened out by the cold?"

"Shouldn't wonder." Robie was busy at his desk, and not in humor for conversation on reminiscent lines. The two old war-dogs at the board had settled down to one of those long, silent struggles which ensue when two champions meet. In the silence which followed, the Judge was looking attentively at the back of the Colonel, and thinking that the old thief was getting about down to skin and bone. He turned with a yawn to Robie, saying:

"This cold weather must take hold of the old Colonel terribly, he's so damnably thin and bald, you know,—bald as a babe. The fact is, the old Colonel ain't long for this world, anyway; think so, Hank?" Robie making no reply, the Judge relapsed into silence for awhile, watching the cat (perilously walking along the edge of the upper shelf) and listening to the occasional hurrying footsteps outside. "I don't know *when* I've seen the windows closed up so, Hank; go down to thirty below to-night; devilish strong wind blowing, too; tough night on the prairies, Hank."

"You bet," replied Hank, briefly.

The Colonel was plainly getting excited. His razor-like back curved sharper than ever as he peered into the intricacies of the board to spy the trap which the fat Squire had set for him. At this point the squeal of boots on the icy walk outside paused, and a moment later Amos Ridings entered, with whiskers covered with ice, and looking like a huge bear in his buffalo coat.

"By Josephus! it's cold," he roared, as he took off his gloves and began to warm his face and hands at the fire.

"Is it?" asked the Judge, comfortably, rising on his tiptoes, only to fall back into his usual attitude legal, legs well spread, shoulders thrown back.

"You bet it is!" replied Amos. "I d'know when I've felt the cold more'n I have t'-day. It's jest snifty; doubles me up like a jack-knife, Judge. How do you stand it?"

"Toler'ble, toler'ble, Amos. But we're agin', we ain't what we were once. Cold takes hold of us."

"That's a fact," answered Amos to the retrospective musings of the Judge. "Time was you an' me would go t' singing-school or sleigh-riding with the girls on a night like this and never notice it."

"Yes, sir; yes, sir!" said the Judge with a sigh. It was a little uncertain in Robie's mind whether the Judge was regretting the lost ability to stand the cold, or the lost pleasure of riding with the girls.

"Great days, those, gentlemen! Lived in Vermont then. Hot-blooded—lungs like an ox. I remember, Sallie Dearborn and I used to go a-foot to singing-school down the valley four miles. But now, wouldn't go riding to-night with the handsomest woman in America, and the best cutter in Rock River."

"Oh! you've got both feet in the grave up t' the ankles, anyway," said Robie, from his desk, but the Judge immovably gazed at the upper shelf on the other side of the room, where the boilers and pans and washboards were stored.

"The Judge is a little on the sentimental order to-night," said Amos.

"Hold on, Colonel! hold on. You've *got* 'o jump. Hah! hah!" roared Gordon from the checker-board. "That's right, that's right!" he ended, as the Colonel complied reluctantly.

"Sock it to the old cuss!" commented Amos. "What I was going to say," he resumed, rolling down the collar of his coat, "was, that when my wife helped me bundle up t'-night, she said I was gitt'n' t' be an old granny. We *are* agin', Judge, the's no denyin' that. We're both gray as Norway rats now. An' speaking of us agin' reminds me,—have y' noticed how bald the old Kyernel's gitt'n'?"

"I have, Amos," answered the Judge, mournfully. "The old man's head is showing age, showing age! Getting thin up there, ain't it?"

The old Colonel bent to his work with studied abstraction, and even when Amos said, judicially, after long scrutiny: "Yes, he'll soon be as bald as a plate," he only lifted one yellow, freckled, bony hand, and brushed his carroty growth of hair across the spot under discussion. Gordon shook his fat paunch in silent laughter, nearly displacing the board.

"I was just telling Robie," pursued Brown, still retaining his reminiscent intonation, "that this storm takes the cake over anything"——

At this point Steve Roach and another fellow entered. Steve was Ridings' hired hand, a herculean fellow, with a drawl, and a liability for taking offense quite as remarkable.

"Say! gents, I'm no spring rooster, but this jest gits away with anything in line of cold *I* ever see."

While this communication was being received in ruminative silence, Steve was holding his ears in his hand and gazing at the intent champions at the board. There they sat; the old Squire panting and wheezing in his excitement, for he was planning a great "snap" on the Colonel, whose red and freckled nose almost touched the board. It was a solemn battle hour. The wind howled mournfully outside, the timbers of the store creaked in the cold, and the huge cannon stove roared in steady bass.

"Speaking about ears," said Steve, after a silence, "dummed if I'd like t' be quite s' bare 'round the ears as Kernel there. I wonder if any o' you fellers has noticed how the ol' feller's lost hair this last summer. He's gittin' bald, they's no coverin' it up—gittin' bald as a plate."

"You're right, Stephen," said the Judge, as he gravely took his stand behind his brother advocate and studied, with the eye of an adept, the field of battle. "We were noticing it when you came in. It's a sad thing, but it must be admitted."

"It's the Kyernel's brains wearin' up through his hair, I take it," commented Amos, as he helped himself to a handful of peanuts out of the bag behind the counter. "Say, Steve, did y' stuff up that hole in front of ol' Barney?"

A shout was heard outside, and then a rush against the door, and immediately two young fellows burst in, followed by a fierce gust of snow. One was Professor Knapp, the other Editor Foster, of the *Morning Call.*

"Well, gents, how's this for high?" said Foster, in a peculiar tone of voice, at which all began to smile. He was a slender fellow with close-clipped, assertive red hair. "In this company we now have the majesty of the law, the power of the press, and the underpinning of the American civilization all represented. Hello! There are a couple of old roosters with their heads together. Gordon, my old enemy, how are you?"

Gordon waved him off with a smile and a wheeze. "Don't bother me now. I've got 'im. I'm laying f'r the old dog. Whist!"

"Got nothing!" snarled the Colonel. "You try that on if you want to. Just swing that man in there if you think it's healthy for him. Just as like as not, you'll slip up on that little trick."

"Ha! Say you so, old True Penny? The Kunnel has met a foeman worthy of his steel," said Foster, in great glee, as he bent above the Colonel. "I know. *How* do I know, quotha? By the curve on the Kunnel's back. The size of the parabola described by that backbone accurately gauges his adversary's skill. But, by the way, gentlemen, have you—but that's a nice point, and I refer all nice points to Professor Knapp. Professor, is it in good taste to make remarks concerning the dress or features of another?"

"Certainly not," answered Knapp, a handsome young fellow with a yellow mustache.

"Not when the person is an esteemed public character, like the Colonel here? What I was about to remark, if it had been proper, was that the old fellow is getting wofully bald. He'll soon be bald as an egg."

"Say!" asked the Colonel, "I want to know how long you're going to keep this thing up? Somebody's dummed sure t' get hurt soon."

"There, there! Colonel," said Brown, soothingly, "don't get excited; you'll lose the rubber. Don't mind 'em. Keep cool."

"Yes, keep cool, Kunnel; it's only our solicitude for your welfare," chipped in Foster. Then, addressing the crowd in a general sort of way, he speculated: "Curious how a man, a plain American citizen like Colonel Peavy, wins a place in the innermost affections of a whole people."

"That's so!" murmured the rest.

"He can't grow bald without deep sympathy from his fellow-citizens. It amounts to a public calamity."

The old Colonel glared in speechless wrath.

"Say! gents," pleaded Gordon, "let up on the old man for the present. He's going to need all of himself if he gets out o' the trap he's in now." He waved his fat hand over the Colonel's head, and smiled blandly at the crowd hugging the stove.

"My head may be bald," grated the old man with a death's-head grin, indescribably ferocious, "but it's got brains enough in it to skunk any man in this crowd three games out o' five."

"The ol' man rather gits the laugh on y' there, gents," called Robie from the other side of the counter. "I hain't seen the old skeesix play better'n he did last night, in years."

"Not since his return from Canada, after the war, I reckon," said Amos, from the kerosene barrel.

"Hold on, Amos," put in the Judge warningly, "that's outlawed. Talking about being bald and the war reminds me of the night Walters and I——— By the way, where is Walters to-night?"

"Sick," put in the Colonel, straightening up exultantly. "I waxed him three straight games last night. You won't see him again till spring. Skunked him once, and beat him twice."

"Oh, git out."

"Hear the old seed twitter!"

"Did you ever notice, gentlemen, how lying and baldness go together?" queried Foster, reflectively.

"No! Do they?"

"Invariably. I've known many colossal liars, and they were all as bald as apples."

The Colonel was getting nervous, and was so slow that even Gordon (who could sit and stare at the board a full half hour without moving) began to be impatient.

"Come, Colonel, marshal your forces a little more promptly. If you're going at me *echelon*, sound y'r bugle; I'm ready."

"Don't worry," answered the Colonel, in his calmest nasal. "I'll accommodate you with all the fight you want."

"Did it ever occur to you," began the Judge again, addressing the crowd generally, as he moved back to the stove and lit another cigar, "did it ever occur to you that it is a little singular a man should get bald on the *top* of his head first? Curious fact. So accustomed to it we no longer wonder at it. Now see the Colonel there. Quite a growth of hair on his clapboarding, as it were, but devilish thin on his roof."

Here the Colonel looked up and tried to say something, but the Judge went on imperturbably:

"Now, I take it that it's strictly providential that a man gets bald on top of his head first, because, if he *must* get bald, it is best to get bald where it can be covered up."

"By jinks, that's a fact!" said Foster, in high admiration of the Judge's ratiocination. Steve was specially pleased, and, drawing a neck-yoke from a barrel standing near, pounded the floor vigorously.

"Talking about being bald," put in Foster, "reminds me of a scheme of mine, which is to send no one out to fight Indians but bald men. Think how powerless they'd be in"——

The talk now drifted off to Indians, politics and religion, edged round to the war, when the grave Judge began telling Ridings and Robie just how "Kilpatrick charged along the Granny White Turnpike," and, on a sheet of wrapping-paper, was showing where Major John Dilrigg fell. "I was on his left, about thirty yards, when I saw him throw up his hand"——

Foster in a low voice was telling something to the Professor and two or three others, which made them whoop with uncontrollable merriment, when the roaring voice of big Sam Walters was heard outside, and a moment later he rolled into the room, filling it with his noise. Lottridge, the watchmaker, and Erlberg, the German baker, came in with him.

"*Hello*, hello, *hello*! All here, are yeh?"

"All here waiting for you—and the turnkey," said Foster.

"Well, here I am. Always on hand, like a sore thumb in huskin' season. What's goin' on here? A game, hey? Hello, Gordon, it's you, is it? Colonel, I owe you several for last night. But what the devil yo' got your cap on fur, Colonel? Ain't it warm enough here for yeh?"

The desperate Colonel, who had snatched up his cap when he heard Walters coming, grinned painfully, pulling his straggly red and white beard nervously. The strain was beginning to tell on his iron nerves. He removed the cap, and with a few muttered words went back to the game, but there was a dangerous gleam in his fishy blue eyes, and the grizzled tufts of red hair above his eyes lowered threateningly. A man who is getting swamped in a game of checkers is not in a mood to bear pleasantly any remarks on his bald head.

"Oh! don't take it off, Colonel," went on his tormentor, hospitably. "When a man gets as old as you are, he's privileged to wear his cap. I wonder if any of you fellers have noticed how the Colonel is shedding his hair."

The old man leaped up, scattering the men on the checkerboard, which flew up and struck Squire Gordon in the face, knocking him off his stool. The old Colonel was ashy pale, and his eyes glared out from under his huge brow like sapphires lit by flame. His spare form, clothed in a seedy Prince Albert frock, towered with a singular dignity. His features worked convulsively a moment, then he burst forth like the explosion of a safety valve:

"Shuttup, damyeh!"

And then the crowd whooped, roared and rolled on the counters and barrels, and roared and whooped again. They stamped and yelled, and ran around like fiends, kicking the boxes and banging the coal scuttle in a perfect pandemonium of mirth, leaving the old man standing there helpless in his wrath, mad enough to shoot. Steve was just preparing to seize the old man from behind, when Squire Gordon, struggling to his feet among the spittoons, cried out, in the voice of a colonel of Fourth of July militia:

"H-O-L-D!"

Silence was restored, and all stood around in expectant attitudes to hear the Squire's explanation. He squared his elbows, shoved up his sleeves, puffed out his fat cheeks, moistened his lips, and began pompously:

"Gentlemen"——

"You've hit it; that's us," said some of the crowd in applause.

"Gentlemen of Rock River, when, in the course of human events, rumor had blow'd to my ears the history of the checker-playing of Rock River, and when I had waxed Cerro Gordo, and Claiborne, and Mower, then, when I say to my ears was borne the clash of resounding arms in Rock River, the emporium of Rock County, then did I yearn for more worlds to conquer, and behold, I buckled on my armor and I am here."

"Behold, he is here," said Foster, in confirmation of the statement. "Good for you, Squire; git breath and go for us some more."

"Hurrah for the Squire," etc.

"I came seekin' whom I might devour, like a raging lion. I sought foeman worthy of my steel. I leaped into the arena and blew my challenge to the four quarters of Rock"——

"Good f'r you! Settemupagin! Go it, you old balloon," they all applauded.

"Knowing my prowess, I sought a fair fout and no favors. I met the enemy, and he was mine. Champion after champion went down before me like— went down like—Ahem! went *down* before me like grass before the mighty cyclone of the Andes."

"Listen to the old blowhard," said Steve.

"Put him out," said the speaker, imperturbably. "Gentlemen, have I the floor?"

"You have," replied Brown, "but come to the point. The Colonel is anxious to begin shooting." The Colonel, who began to suspect himself victimized, stood wondering what under heaven they were going to do next.

"I am a-gitt'n' there," said the orator with a broad and sunny condescension. "I found your champions an' laid 'em low. I waxed Walters, and then I tackled the Colonel. I tried the *echelon*, the 'general advance,' then the 'give away' and 'flank' movements. But the Colonel *was there!* Till this last game it was a fair field and no favor. And now, gentlemen of Rock, I desire t' state to my deeply respected opponent that he is still champion of Rock, and I'm not sure but of Northern Iowa."

"Three cheers for the Kunnel!"

And while they were being given the Colonel's brows relaxed, and the champion of Cerro Gordo continued earnestly:

"And now I wish to state to Colonel the solemn fact that I had nothing to do with the job put up on him to-night. I scorn to use such means in a battle. Colonel, you may be as bald as an apple, or an egg, yes, or a *plate*, but you can play more checkers than any man I ever met; more checkers than any other man on God's green footstool. With one single, lone exception— myself."

At this moment, somebody hit the Squire from Cerro Gordo with a decayed apple, and as the crowd shouted and groaned Robie turned down the lights on the tumult. The old Colonel seized the opportunity for putting a handful of salt down Walters' neck, and slipped out of the door like a ghost. As the crowd swarmed out on the icy walk, Editor Foster yelled:

"Gents! let me give you a pointer. Keep your eye peeled for the next edition of the Rock River *Morning Call*."

And the bitter wind swept away the answering shouts of the pitiless gang.

Part VII.

DRIFTING CRANE
THE INDIAN AND THE PIONEER.

Before them, surely, sullenly and slow,
The desperate and cheated Indians go.

DRIFTING CRANE.

THE people of Boomtown invariably spoke of Henry Wilson as the oldest settler in the Jim Valley, as he was of Buster County; but the Eastern man, with his ideas of an "old settler," was surprised as he met the short, silent, middle-aged man, who was very loath to tell anything about himself, and about whom many strange and thrilling stories were told by good story-tellers. In 1879 he was the only settler in the upper part of the valley, living alone on the banks of the Elm, a slow, tortuous stream pulsing lazily down the valley, too small to be called a river and too long to be called a creek. For two years, it is said, Wilson had only the company of his cattle, especially during the winter-time, and now and then a visit from an Indian, or a trapper after mink and musk-rats.

Between his ranch and the settlements in Eastern Dakota there was the wedge-shaped reservation known as the Sisseton Indian Reserve, on which were stationed the customary agency and company of soldiers. But, of course, at that time the Indians were not restricted closely to the bounds of the reserve, but ranged freely over the vast and beautiful prairie lying between the coteaux or ranges of low hills which mark out "the Jim Valley." The valley was unsurveyed for the most part, and the Indians naturally felt a sort of proprietorship in it, and when Wilson drove his cattle down into the valley and squatted, the chief, Drifting Crane, welcomed him, as a host might, to an abundant feast whose hospitality was presumed upon, but who felt the need of sustaining his reputation as a host, and submitted graciously.

The Indians during the first summer got to know Wilson, and liked him for his silence, his courage, his generosity; but the older men pondered upon the matter a great deal and watched with grave faces to see him ploughing up the sod for his garden. There was something strange in this solitary man thus deserting his kindred, coming here to live alone with his cattle; they could not understand it. What they said in those pathetic, dimly lighted lodges will never be known; but when winter came, and the new-comer did not drive his cattle back over the hills as they thought he would, then the old chieftains took long counsel upon it. Night after night they smoked upon it, and at last Drifting Crane said to two of his young men: "Go ask this cattleman why he remains in the cold and snow with his cattle. Ask him why he does not drive his cattle home."

This was in March, and one evening a couple of days later, as Wilson was about re-entering his shanty at the close of his day's work, he was confronted by two stalwart Indians, who greeted him pleasantly.

"How d'e do? How d'e do?" he said in reply. "Come in. Come in and take a snack."

The Indians entered and sat silently while he put some food on the table. They hardly spoke till after they had eaten. The Indian is always hungry, for the reason that his food supply is insufficient and his clothing poor. When they sat on the cracker-boxes and soap-boxes which served as seats, they spoke. They told him of the chieftain's message. They said they had come to assist him in driving his cattle back across the hills; that he must go.

To all this talk in the Indian's epigrammatic way, and in the dialect which has never been written, the rancher replied almost as briefly: "You go back and tell Drifting Crane that I like this place; that I'm here to stay; that I don't want any help to drive my cattle. I'm on the lands of the Great Father at Washington, and Drifting Crane ain't got any say about it. Now that sizes the whole thing up. I ain't got anything against you nor against him, but I'm a settler; that's my constitution; and now I'm settled I'm going to stay."

While the Indians discussed his words between themselves he made a bed of blankets on the floor and said: "I never turn anybody out. A white man is just as good as an Indian as long as he behaves himself as well. You can bunk here."

The Indians didn't understand his words fully, but they did understand his gesture, and they smiled and accepted the courtesy, so like their own rude hospitality. Then they all smoked a pipe of tobacco in silence, and at last Wilson turned in and went serenely off to sleep, hearing the mutter of the Indians lying before the fire.

In the morning he gave them as good a breakfast as he had—bacon and potatoes, with coffee and crackers. Then he shook hands, saying: "Come again. I ain't got anything against you. You've done y'r duty. Now go back and tell your chief what I've said. I'm at home every day. Good day."

The Indians smiled kindly, and drawing their blankets over their arms, went away toward the east.

During April and May two or three reconnoitering parties of land-hunters drifted over the hills and found him out. He was glad to see them, for, to tell the truth, the solitude of his life was telling on him. The winter had been severe, and he had hardly caught a glimpse of a white face during the three midwinter months, and his provisions were scanty.

These parties brought great news. One of them was the advance surveying party for a great Northern railroad, and they said a line of road was to be surveyed during the summer if their report was favorable.

"Well, what d'ye think of it?" Wilson asked, with a smile.

"Think! It's immense!" said a small man in the party, whom the rest called Judge Balser. "Why, they'll be a town of four thousand inhabitants in this valley before snow flies. We'll send the surveyors right over the divide next month."

They sent some papers to Wilson a few weeks later, which he devoured as a hungry dog might devour a plate of bacon. The papers were full of the wonderful resources of the Jim Valley. It spoke of the nutritious grasses for stock. It spoke of the successful venture of the lonely settler Wilson, how his stock fattened upon the winter grasses without shelter, etc., what vegetables he grew, etc., etc.

Wilson was reading this paper for the sixth time one evening in May. He had laid off his boots, his pipe was freshly filled, and he sat in the doorway in vast content, unmindful of the glory of color that filled the western sky, and the superb evening chorus of the prairie-chickens, holding conventions on every hillock. He felt something touch him on the shoulder, and looked up to see a tall Indian gazing down upon him with a look of strange pride and gravity. Wilson sprang to his feet and held out his hand.

"Drifting Crane, how d'e do?"

The Indian bowed, but did not take the settler's hand. Drifting Crane would have been called old if he had been a white man, and there was a look of age in the fixed lines of his powerful, strongly modeled face, but no suspicion of weakness in the splendid poise of his broad, muscular body. There was a smileless gravity about his lips and eyes which was very impressive.

"I'm glad to see you. Come in and get something to eat," said Wilson, after a moment's pause.

The chief entered the cabin and took a seat near the door. He took a cup of milk and some meat and bread silently, and ate while listening to the talk of the settler.

"I don't brag on my biscuits, chief, but they *eat*, if a man is hungry enough. An' the milk's all right. I suppose you've come to see why I ain't moseying back over the divide?"

The chief, after a long pause, began to speak in a low, slow voice, as if choosing his words. He spoke in broken English, of course, but his speech was very direct and plain, and had none of those absurd figures of rhetoric which romancers invariably put into the mouths of Indians. His voice was almost lion-like in its depth, and yet was not unpleasant. It was easy to see that he was a chief by virtue of his own personality.

"Cattleman, my young men brought me bad message from you. They brought your words to me, saying he will not go away."

"That's about the way the thing stands," replied Wilson, in response to the question that was in the old chief's steady eyes. "I'm here to stay. This ain't your land. This is Uncle Sam's land, and part of it'll be mine as soon as the surveyors come to measure it off."

"Who gave it away?" asked the chief. "My people were cheated out of it. They didn't know what they were doing."

"I can't help that. That's for Congress to say. That's the business of the Great Father at Washington." Wilson's voice changed. He knew and liked the chief; he didn't want to offend him. "They ain't no use making a fuss, chief. You won't gain anything."

There was a look of deep sorrow in the old man's face. At last he spoke again: "The cattleman is welcome; but he must go, because whenever one white man goes and calls it good, the others come. Drifting Crane has seen it far in the east, twice. The white men come thick as the grass. They tear up the sod. They build houses. They scare the buffalo away. They spoil my young men with whisky. Already they begin to climb the eastern hills. Soon they will fill the valley, and Drifting Crane and his people will be surrounded. The sod will all be black."

"I hope you're right," was the rancher's grim reply.

"But they will not come if the cattleman go back to say the water is not good. There is no grass, and the Indians own the land."

Wilson smiled at the childish faith of the chief. "Won't do, chief—won't do. That won't do any good. I might as well stay."

The chief rose. He was touched by the settler's laugh; his eyes flashed; his voice took on a sterner note. "The white man *must* go!"

Wilson rose also. He was not a large man, but he was a very resolute one. "I shan't go!" he said, through his clinched teeth. Each man understood the tones of the other perfectly.

It was a thrilling, a significant scene. It was in absolute truth the meeting of the modern vidette of civilization with one of the rear-guard of retreating barbarism. Each man was a type; each was wrong, and each was right. The Indian as true and noble from the barbaric point of view as the white man. He was a warrior and hunter—made so by circumstances over which he had no control. Guiltless as the panther, because war to a savage is the necessity of life.

The settler represented the unflagging energy and fearless heart of the American pioneer. Narrow-minded, partly brutalized by hard labor and a lonely life, yet an admirable figure for all that. As he looked into the Indian's face he seemed to grow in height. He felt behind him all the weight of the millions of westward-moving settlers; he stood the representative of an unborn State. He took down a rifle from the wall—the magazine rifle, most modern of guns; he patted the stock, pulled the crank, throwing a shell into view.

"You know this thing, chief?"

The Indian nodded slightly.

"Well, I'll go when—this—is—empty."

"But my young men are many."

"So are the white men—my brothers."

The chief's head dropped forward. Wilson, ashamed of his boasting, put the rifle back on the wall.

"I'm not here to fight. You can kill me any time. You could 'a' killed me to-night, but it wouldn't do any good. It 'ud only make it worse for you. Why, they'll be a town in here bigger'n all your tribe before two grass from now. It ain't no use, Drifting Crane; it's *got* to be. You an' I can't help n'r hinder it. I know just how you feel about it, but I tell yeh it ain't no use to fight."

Drifting Crane turned his head and gazed out on the western sky, still red with the light of the fallen sun. His face was rigid as bronze, but there was a dreaming, prophetic look in his eyes. A lump came into the settler's throat; for the first time in his life he got a glimpse of the infinite despair of the Indian. He forgot that Drifting Crane was the representative of a "vagabond race;" he saw in him, or rather *felt* in him, something almost magnetic. He was a *man*, and a man of sorrows. The settler's voice was husky when he spoke again, and his lips trembled.

"Chief, I'd go to-morrow if it 'ud do any good, but it won't—not a particle. You know that, when you stop to think a minute. What good did it do to massa*cree* all them settlers at New Ulm? What good will it do to murder me and a hundred others? Not a bit. A thousand others would take our places.

So I might just as well stay, and we might just as well keep good friends. Killin' is out o' fashion; don't do any good."

There was a twitching about the stern mouth of the Indian chief. He understood all too well the irresistible logic of the pioneer. He kept his martial attitude, but his broad chest heaved painfully, and his eyes grew dim. At last he said: "Good-by. Cattleman right; Drifting Crane wrong. Shake hands. Good-by." He turned and strode away.

The rancher watched him till he mounted his pony, picketed down by the river; watched him as, with drooping head and rein flung loose upon the neck of his horse, he rode away into the dusk, hungry, weary and despairing, to face his problem alone. Again, for the thousandth time, the impotence of the Indian's arm and the hopelessness of his fate were shown as perfectly as if two armies had met and soaked the beautiful prairie sod with blood.

"This is all wrong," muttered the settler. "There's land enough for us all, or ought to be. I don't understand——Well, I'll leave it to Uncle Sam anyway." He ended with a sigh.

PART VIII.

OLD DADDY DEERING
THE COUNTRY FIDDLER.

Like Scotland's harper,
Or Irish piper, with his droning lays,
Before the spread of modern life and light
The country fiddler slowly disappears.

DADDY DEERING.

I.

THEY were threshing on Farmer Jennings' place when Daddy made his very characteristic appearance. Milton, a boy of thirteen, was gloomily holding sacks for the measurer, and the glory of the October day was dimmed by the suffocating dust, and poisoned by the smarting beards and chaff which had worked their way down his neck. The bitterness of the dreaded task was deepened also by contrast with the gambols of his cousin Billy, who was hunting rats with Growler amid the last sheaves of the stack bottom. The piercing shrieks of Billy, as he clapped his hands in murderous glee, mingled now and again with the barking of the dog.

The machine seemed to fill the world with its snarling boom, which became a deafening yell when the cylinder ran empty for a moment. It was nearly noon, and the men were working silently, with occasional glances toward the sun to see how near dinner-time it was. The horses, dripping with sweat, and with patches of foam under their harness, moved round and round steadily to the cheery whistle of the driver.

The wild, imperious song of the bell-metal cog-wheel had sung into Milton's ears till it had become a torture, and every time he lifted his eyes to the beautiful far-off sky, where the clouds floated like ships, a lump of rebellious anger rose in his throat. Why should he work in this choking dust and deafening noise while the hawks could sail and sweep from hill to hill with nothing to do but play?

Occasionally his uncle, the feeder, smiled down upon him, his face black as a negro, great goggles of glass and wire-cloth covering his merry eyes. His great good-nature shone out in the flash of his white teeth, behind his dusky beard, and he tried to encourage Milton with his smile. He seemed tireless to the other hands. He was so big and strong. He had always been Milton's boyish hero. So Milton crowded back the tears that came into his eyes, and would not let his uncle see how childish he was.

A spectator riding along the road would have remarked upon the lovely setting for this picturesque scene—the low swells of prairie, shrouded with faint, misty light from the unclouded sky, the flaming colors of the trees, the faint sound of cow-bells, and the cheery sound of the machine. But to be a tourist and to be a toiler in a scene like this are quite different things.

They were anxious to finish the setting by noon, and so the feeder was crowding the cylinder to its limit, rolling the grain in with slow and apparently effortless swaying from side to side, half-buried in the loose yellow straw. But about eleven o'clock the machine came to a stand, to wait while a broken tooth was being replaced, and Milton fled from the terrible dust beside the measuring-spout, and was shaking the chaff out of his clothing, when he heard a high, snappy, nasal voice call down from the straw-pile. A tall man, with a face completely masked in dust, was speaking to Mr. Jennings:

"Say, young man, I guess you'll haf to send another man up here. It's poorty stiff work f'r two; yes, sir, poorty stiff."

"There, there! I thought you'd cry 'cavy,'" laughed Mr. Jennings. "I told you it wasn't the place for an old man."

"Old man," snarled the figure in the straw. "I ain't so old but I can daown you, sir—yessir, condemmit, yessir!"

"I'm your man," replied Jennings, smiling up at him.

The man rolled down the side of the stack, disappearing in a cloud of dust and chaff. When he came to light, Milton saw a tall, gaunt old man of sixty years of age, or older. Nothing could be seen but a dusty expanse of face, ragged beard, and twinkling, sharp little eyes. His color was lost, his eyes half hid. Without waiting for ceremony, the men clinched. The crowd roared with laughter, for though Jennings was the younger, the older man was a giant still, and the struggle lasted for some time. He made a gallant fight, but his breath gave out, and he lay at last flat on his back.

"I wish I was your age, young man," he said ruefully, as he rose. "I'd knock the heads o' these young scamps t'gether—yessir!—I could do it, too!".

"Talk's a good dog, uncle," said a young man.

The old man turned on him so ferociously that he fled.

"Run, condemn yeh! I own y' can beat me at that."

His face was not unpleasant, though his teeth were mainly gone, and his skin the color of leather and wrinkled as a pan of cream. His eyes had a certain sparkle of fun that belied his rasping voice, which seemed to have the power to lift a boy clean off his feet. His frame was bent and thin, but of great height and breadth, bony and tough as hickory. At some far time vast muscles must have rolled on those giant limbs, but toil had bent and stiffened him.

"Never been sick a day 'n my life; no, sir!" he said, in his rapid, rasping, emphatic way, as they were riding across the stubble to dinner. "And by gol! I c'n stand as long at the tail of a stacker as any man, sir. Dummed if I turn my hand for any man in the State; no, sir; no, sir! But if I do two men's works, I am goin' to have two men's pay—that's all, sir!"

Jennings laughed and said: "All right, uncle. I'll send another man up there this afternoon."

The old man seemed to take a morbid delight in the hard and dirty places, and his endurance was marvelous. He could stand all day at the tail of a stacker, tirelessly pushing the straw away with an indifferent air, as if it were all mere play.

He measured the grain the next day, because it promised to be a noisier and dustier job than working in the straw, and it was in this capacity that Milton came to know and to hate him, and to associate him with that most hated of all tasks, the holding of sacks. To a twelve-year-old boy it seems to be the worst job in the world.

All day while the hawks wheel and dip in the glorious air, and the trees glow like banks of roses; all day, while the younger boys are tumbling about the sun-lit straw, to be forced to stand holding sacks, like a convict, was maddening. Daddy, whose rugged features, bent shoulders and ragged cap loomed through the suffocating, blinding dust, necessarily came to seem like the jailer who held the door to freedom.

And when the dust and noise and monotony seemed the very hardest to bear the old man's cackling laugh was sure to rise above the howl of the cylinder.

"Nem mind, sonny! Chaff ain't pizen; dust won't hurt ye a mite." And when Milton was unable to laugh the old man tweaked his ear with his leathery thumb and finger.

Then he shouted long, disconnected yarns, to which Milton could make neither head nor tail, and which grew at last to be inaudible to him, just as the steady boom and snarl of the great machine did. Then he fell to studying the old man's clothes, which were a wonder to him. He spent a good deal of time trying to discover which were the original sections of the coat, and especially of the vest, which was ragged and yellow with age, with the cotton-batting working out; and yet Daddy took the greatest care of it, folding it carefully and putting it away during the heat of the day out of reach of the crickets.

One of his peculiarities, as Mrs. Jennings learned on the second day, was his habit of coming to breakfast. But he always earned all he got, and more too; and, as it was probable that his living at home was frugal, Mrs.

Jennings smiled at his thrift, and quietly gave him his breakfast if he arrived late, which was not often.

He had bought a little farm not far away, and settled down into a mode of life which he never afterward changed. As he was leaving at the end of the third day, he said:

"Now, sir; if you want any bootcherin' done, I'm y'r man. I don't turn m' hand over f'r any man in the State; no, sir! I c'n git a hawg on the gambrils jest a leetle quicker'n any other man I ever see; yes, sir; by gum!"

"All right, uncle; I'll send for you when I'm ready to kill."

II.

HOG-KILLING was one of the events of a boy's life on a Western farm, and Daddy was destined to be associated in the minds of Shep and Milton with another disagreeable job, that of building the fire and carrying water.

It was very early on a keen, biting morning in November when Daddy came driving into the yard with his rude, long-runnered sled, one horse half his length behind the other in spite of the driver's clucking. He was delighted to catch the boys behind in the preparation.

"A-a-h-h-r-r-h-h!" he rasped out, "you lazy vagabon's? Why ain't you got that fire blazin'? WHAT the devil do y' mean, you rascals! Here it is broad daylight, and that fire not built. I vum, sir, you need a thrashin', the whole kit an bilun' of ye; yessir! Come, come, come! hustle now, stir your boots! hustle y'r boots—Ha! ha! ha!"

It was of no use to plead cold weather and damp chips.

"What has that got to do with it, sir? I vum, sir, when I was your age, I could make a fire of green red-oak; yessir! Don't talk to me of colds! Stir your stumps and get warm, sir!"

The old man put up his horses (and fed them generously with oats), and then went to the house to ask for "a leetle something hot—mince pie or sassidge." His request was very modest, but, as a matter of fact, he sat down and ate a very hearty breakfast, while the boys worked away at the fire under the big kettle.

The hired man, under Daddy's direction, drew the bob-sleighs into position on the sunny side of the corn-crib, and arranged the barrel at the proper slant while the old man ground his knives, Milton turning the grindstone— another hateful task, which Daddy's stories could not alleviate.

Daddy never finished a story. If he started in to tell about a horse-trade, it infallibly reminded him of a cattle trade, and talking of cattle switched him off upon logging, and logging reminded him of some heavy snow-storms he had known. Each parenthesis outgrew its proper limits, till he forgot what should have been the main story. His stories had some compensation, for when he stopped to try to recollect where he was, the pressure on the grindstone was released.

At last the water was hot, and the time came to seize the hogs. This was the old man's great moment. He stood in the pen and shrieked with laughter while the hired men went rolling, one after the other, upon the ground, or were bruised against the fence by the rush of the burly swine.

"You're a fine lot," he laughed. "Now, then, sir, *grab 'im*! Why don't ye nail 'im? I vum, sir, if I couldn't do better'n that, sir, I'd sell out; I would, sir, by gol! Get out o' the way!"

With a lofty scorn he waved aside all help and stalked like a gladiator toward the pigs huddled in one corner of the pen. And when the selected victim was rushing by him, his long arm and great bony hand swept out, caught him by the ear and flung him upon his side, squealing with deafening shrillness. But in spite of his smiling concealment of effort, Daddy had to lean against the fence and catch his breath even while he boasted:

"I'm an old codger, sir, but I'm worth—a dozen o' you—spindle-legged chaps; dum me if I ain't, sir!"

His pride in his ability to catch and properly kill a hog was as genuine as the old knight-errant's pride in his ability to stick a knife into another steel-clothed brigand like himself. When the slain shote was swung upon the planking on the sled before the barrel, Daddy rested, while the boys filled the barrel with water from the kettle.

There was always a weird charm about this stage of the work to the boys. The sun shone warm and bright in the lee of the corn-crib; the steam rose up, white and voluminous, from the barrel; the eaves dropped steadily; the hens ventured near, nervously, but full of curiosity, while the men laughed and joked with Daddy, starting him off on long stories, and winking at each other when his back was turned.

At last he mounted his planking, selecting Mr. Jennings to pull upon the other handle of the hog-hook. He considered he conferred a distinct honor in this selection.

"The time's been, sir, when I wouldn't thank any man for his help. No, sir, wouldn't thank 'im."

"What do you do with these things?" asked one of the men, kicking two iron candlesticks which the old man laid conveniently near.

"Scrape a hawg with them, sir? What did y' s'pose, you numbskull?"

"Well, I never saw anything"——

"You'll have a chance mighty quick, sir. Grab ahold, sir! Swing 'im around—there! Now easy, easy! Now, then, one, two; one, two—that's right."

While he dipped the porker in the water, pulling with his companion rhythmically upon the hook, he talked incessantly, mixing up scraps of stories and boastings of what he could do, with commands of what he wanted the other man to do.

"The best man I ever worked with. *Now turn 'im, turn 'im!*" he yelled, reaching over Jennings' wrist. "Grab under my wrist. There! won't ye never learn how to turn a hawg? *Now, out with 'im!*" was his next wild yell, as the steaming hog was jerked out of the water upon the planking. "Now try the hair on them ears! Beautiful scald," he said, clutching his hand full of bristles and beaming with pride. "Never see anything finer. Here, Bub, a pail of hot water, quick! Try one of them candlesticks! They ain't no better scraper than the bottom of an old iron candlestick; no, sir! Dum your new-fangled scrapers! I made a bet once with old Jake Ridgeway that I could scrape the hair off'n two hawgs, by gum, quicker'n he could one. Jake was blowin' about a new scraper he had …

"Yes, yes, yes, dump it right into the barrel. Condemmit! Ain't you got no gumption?... So Sim Smith, he held the watch. Sim was a mighty good hand t' work with; he was about the only man I ever sawed with who didn't ride the saw. He could jerk a cross-cut saw.... Now let him in again, now; *he-ho*, once again! *Roll him over now*, that foreleg needs a tech o' water. Now out with him again; that's right, that's right! By gol, a beautiful scald as ever I see!"

Milton, standing near, caught his eye again. "Clean that ear, sir! What the devil you standin' there for?" He returned to his story after a pause. "A—n—d Jake he scraped away—*Hyare*," he shouted, suddenly, "don't ruggle the skin like that! Can't you see the way I do it? Leave it smooth as a baby, sir—yessir!"

He worked on in this way all day, talking unceasingly, never shirking a hard job, and scarcely showing fatigue at any moment.

"I'm short o' breath a leetle, that's all; never git tired, but my wind gives out. Dum cold got on me, too."

He ate a huge supper of liver and potatoes, still working away hard at an ancient horse-trade, and when he drove off at night, he had not yet finished a single one of the dozen stories he had begun.

III.

BUT pitching grain and hog-killing were on the lower levels of his art, for above all else Daddy loved to be called upon to play the fiddle for dances. He "officiated" for the first time at a dance given by one of the younger McTurgs. They were all fiddlers themselves—had been for three generations—but they seized the opportunity of helping Daddy and at the same time of relieving themselves of the trouble of furnishing the music while the rest danced.

Milton attended this dance, and saw Daddy for the first time earning his money pleasantly. From that time on the associations around his personality were less severe, and they came to like him better. He came early, with his old fiddle in a time-worn white-pine box. His hair was neatly combed to the top of his long, narrow head, and his face was very clean. The boys all greeted him with great pleasure, and asked him where he would sit.

"Right on that table, sir; put a chair up there."

He took his chair on the kitchen-table as if it were a throne. He wore huge moccasins of moose-hide on his feet, and for special occasions like this added a paper collar to his red woolen shirt. He took off his coat and laid it across his chair for a cushion. It was all very funny to the young people, but they obeyed him laughingly, and while they "formed on," he sawed his violin and coaxed it up to concert pitch, and twanged it and banged it into proper tunefulness.

"A-a-a-ll-ready there!" he rasped out, with prodigious force. "Everybody git into his place!" Then, lifting one huge foot, he put the fiddle under his chin, and, raising his bow till his knuckles touched the strings, he yelled, "Already, G'LANG!" and brought his foot down with a startling bang on the first note. *Rye doodle doo, doodle doo.*

As he went on and the dancers fell into rhythm, the clatter of heavy boots seemed to thrill him with old-time memories, and he kept boisterous time with his foot while his high, rasping nasal rang high above the confusion of tongues and heels and swaying forms.

"*Ladies'* gran' change! FOUR hands round! *Bal*-ance all! *Elly*-man left! Back to play-cis."

His eyes closed in a sort of intoxication of pleasure, but he saw all that went on in some miraculous way.

"*First* lady lead to the right—*toodle rum rum! Gent* foller after (step along thar)! Four hands round"——

The boys were immensely pleased with him. They delighted in his antics rather than in his tunes, which were exceedingly few and simple. They seemed never to be able to get enough of one tune which he called "Honest John," and which he played in his own way, accompanied by a chant which he meant, without doubt, to be musical.

"HON-ers tew your pardners—*tee teedle deedle dee dee dee dee!* Stand up straight an' put on your style! *Right* an' left four"——

The hat was passed by the floor-manager during the evening, and Daddy got nearly three dollars, which delighted Milton very much.

At supper he insisted on his prerogative, which was to take the prettiest girl out to supper.

"Look-a-here, Daddy, ain't that crowdin' the mourners?" objected the others.

"What do you mean by that, sir? No, sir! Always done it, in Michigan and Yark State both; yes, sir."

He put on his coat ceremoniously, while the tittering girls stood about the room waiting. He did not delay. His keen eyes had made selection long before, and, approaching Rose Watson with old-fashioned, elaborate gallantry, he said: "*May* I have the pleasure?" and marched out triumphantly, amidst shouts of laughter.

His shrill laugh rang high above the rest at the table, as he said: "I'm the youngest man in this crowd, sir! Demmit, I bet a hat I c'n dance down any man in this crowd; yes, sir. The old man can do it yet."

They all took sides in order to please him.

"I'll bet he can," said Hugh McTurg; "I'll bet a dollar on Daddy."

"I'll take the bet," said Joe Randall, and with great noise the match was arranged to come the first thing after supper.

"All right, sir; any time, sir. I'll let you know the old man is on earth yet."

While the girls were putting away the supper dishes, the young man lured Daddy out into the yard for a wrestling-match, but some of the others objected.

"Oh, now, that won't do! If Daddy was a young man"——

"What do you mean, sir? I am young enough for you, sir. Just let me get ahold o' you, sir, and I'll show you, you young rascal! you dem jackanapes!" he ended, almost shrieking with rage, as he shook his fist in the face of his grinning tormentors.

The others held him back with much apparent alarm, and ordered the other fellows away.

"There, there, Daddy, I wouldn't mind him! I wouldn't dirty my hands on him; he ain't worth it. Just come inside, and we'll have that dancing-match now."

Daddy reluctantly returned to the house, and, having surrendered his violin to Hugh McTurg, was ready for the contest. As he stepped into the middle of the room he was not altogether ludicrous. His rusty trousers were bagged at the knee, and his red woolen stockings showed between the tops of his moccasins and his pantaloon-legs; and his coat, utterly characterless as to color and cut, added to the stoop in his shoulders, and yet there was a rude sort of grace and a certain dignity about his bearing which kept down laughter. They were to have a square dance of the old-fashioned sort.

"*Farrm* on," he cried, and the fiddler struck out the first note of the Virginia Reel. Daddy led out Rose, and the dance began. He straightened up till his tall form towered above the rest of the boys like a weather-beaten pine-tree, as he balanced and swung and led and called off the changes with a voice full of imperious command.

The fiddler took a malicious delight toward the last in quickening the time of the good old dance, and that put the old man on his mettle.

"Go it, ye young rascal!" he yelled. He danced like a boy and yelled like a demon, catching a laggard here and there, and hurling them into place like tops, while he kicked and stamped, wound in and out and waved his hands in the air with a gesture which must have dated back to the days of Washington. At last, flushed, breathless, but triumphant, he danced a final break-down to the tune of "Leather Breeches," to show he was unsubdued.

IV.

BUT these rare days passed away. As the country grew older it lost the wholesome simplicity of pioneer days, and Daddy got a chance to play but seldom. He no longer pleased the boys and girls—his music was too monotonous and too simple. He felt this very deeply. Once in a while he broke out to some of the old neighbors in protest against the changes.

"The boys I used to trot on m' knee are gittin' too high-toned. They wouldn't be found dead with old Deering, and then the preachers are gittin' thick, and howlin' agin dancin', and the country's filling up with Dutchmen, so't I'm left out."

As a matter of fact, there were few homes now where Daddy could sit on the table, in his ragged vest and rusty pantaloons, and play "Honest John," while the boys thumped about the floor. There were few homes where the old man was even a welcome visitor, and he felt this rejection keenly. The women got tired of seeing him about, because of his uncleanly habits of spitting and his tiresome stories. Many of the old neighbors had died or moved away, and the young people had gone West or to the cities. Men began to pity him rather than laugh at him, which hurt him more than their ridicule. They began to favor him at threshing or at the fall hog-killing.

"Oh, you're getting old, Daddy; you'll have to give up this heavy work. Of course, if you feel able to do it, why, all right! Like to have you do it, but I guess we'll have to have a man to do the heavy lifting, I s'pose."

"I s'pose not, sir! I am jest as able to yank a hawg as ever, sir; yes, sir, demmit—demmit! Do you think I've got one foot in the grave?"

Nevertheless, Daddy often failed to come to time on appointed days, and it was painful to hear him trying to explain, trying to make light of it all.

"M' caugh wouldn't let me sleep last night. A gol-dum leetle, nasty, ticklin' caugh, too; but it kept me awake, fact was, an'—well, m' wife, she said I hadn't better come. But don't you worry, sir; it won't happen again, sir; no, sir."

His hands got stiffer year by year, and his simple tunes became practically a series of squeaks and squalls. There came a time when the fiddle was laid away almost altogether, for his left hand got caught in the cog-wheels of the horse-power, and all four of the fingers on that hand were crushed. Thereafter he could only twang a little on the strings. It was not long after this that he struck his foot with the ax and lamed himself for life.

As he lay groaning in bed, Mr. Jennings went in to see him and tried to relieve the old man's feelings by telling him the number of times he had practically cut his feet off, and said he knew it was a terrible hard thing to put up with.

"Gol dummit, it ain't the pain," the old sufferer yelled, "it's the dum awkwardness. I've chopped all my life; I can let an ax in up to the maker's name, and hew to a hair-line; yes, sir! It was jest them dum new mittens my wife made; they was s' slippery," he ended, with a groan.

As a matter of fact, the one accident hinged upon the other. It was the failure of his left hand, with its useless fingers, to do its duty, that brought the ax down upon his foot. The pain was not so much physical as mental. To think that he, who could hew to a hair-line, right and left hand, should cut his own foot like a ten-year-old boy—that scared him. It brought age and decay close to him. For the first time in his life he felt that he was fighting a losing battle.

A man like this lives so much in the flesh that when his limbs begin to fail him, everything else seems slipping away. He had gloried in his strength. He had exulted in the thrill of his life-blood and in the swell of his vast muscles; he had clung to the idea that he was strong as ever, till this last blow came upon him, and then he began to think and to tremble.

When he was able to crawl about again, he was not the same man. He was gloomy and morose, snapping and snarling at all that came near him, like a wounded bear. He was alone a great deal of the time during the winter following his hurt. Neighbors seldom went in, and for weeks he saw no one but his hired hand, and the faithful, dumb little old woman, his wife, who moved about without any apparent concern or sympathy for his suffering. The hired hand, whenever he called upon the neighbors, or whenever questions were asked, said that Daddy hung around over the stove most of the time, paying no attention to any one or anything. "He ain't dangerous 'tall," he said, meaning that Daddy was not dangerously ill.

Milton rode out from school one winter day with Bill, the hand, and was so much impressed with his story of Daddy's condition that he rode home with him. He found the old man sitting bent above the stove, wrapped in a quilt, shivering and muttering to himself. He hardly looked up when Milton spoke to him, and seemed scarcely to comprehend what he said.

Milton was much alarmed at the terrible change, for the last time he had seen him he had towered above him, laughingly threatening to "warm his jacket," and now here he sat, a great hulk of flesh, his mind flickering and flaring under every wind of suggestion, soon to go out altogether.

 In reply to questions he only muttered with a trace of his old spirit: "I'm all right. Jest as good a man as I ever was, only I'm cold. I'll be all right when spring comes, so 't I c'n git outdoors. Somethin' to warm me up, yessir; I'm cold, that's all."

The young fellow sat in awe before him, but the old wife and Bill moved about the room, taking very little interest in what the old man said or did. Bill at last took down the violin. "I'll wake him up," he said. "This always fetches the old feller. Now watch 'im."

"Oh, don't do that!" Milton said, in horror. But Bill drew the bow across the strings in the same way that Daddy always did when tuning up.

He lifted his head as Bill dashed into "Honest John," in spite of Milton's protest. He trotted his feet after a little and drummed with his hands on the arms of his chair, then smiled a little in a pitiful way. Finally he reached out his right hand for the violin and took it into his lap. He tried to hold the neck with his poor, old, mutilated left hand and burst into tears.

"Don't you do that again, Bill," Milton said. "It's better for him to forget that. Now you take the best care of him you can to-night. I don't think he's going to live long; I think you ought to go for the doctor right off."

"Oh, he's been like this for the last two weeks; he ain't sick, he's jest old, that's all," replied Bill, brutally.

And the old lady, moving about without passion and without speech, seemed to confirm this; and yet Milton was unable to get the picture of the old man out of his mind. He went home with a great lump in his throat.

The next morning, while they were at breakfast, Bill burst wildly into the room.

"Come over there, all of you; we want you."

They all looked up much scared. "What's the matter, Bill?"

"Daddy's killed himself," said Bill, and turned to rush back, followed by Mr. Jennings and Milton.

While on the way across the field Bill told how it all happened.

"He wouldn't go to bed, the old lady couldn't make him, and when I got up this morning I didn't think nothin' about it. I s'posed, of course, he'd gone to bed all right, but when I was going out to the barn I stumbled across something in the snow, and I felt around, and there he was. He got hold of my revolver someway. It was on the shelf by the washstand, and I s'pose he went out there so 't we wouldn't hear him." "I dassn't touch him," he said, with a shiver; "and the old woman, she jest slumped down in a chair an set there—wouldn't do a thing—so I come over to see you."

Milton's heart swelled with remorse. He felt guilty because he had not gone directly for the doctor. To think that the old sufferer had killed himself was horrible and seemed impossible.

The wind was blowing the snow, cold and dry, across the yard, but the sun shone brilliantly upon the figure in the snow as they came up to it. There Daddy lay. The snow was in his scant hair and in the hollow of his vast, half-naked chest. A pistol was in his hand, but there was no mark upon him, and Milton's heart leaped with quick relief. It was delirium, not suicide.

There was a sort of majesty in the figure half-buried in the snow. His hands were clenched, and there was a frown of resolution on his face, as if he had fancied Death coming and had gone defiantly forth to meet him.

PART IX.

THE SOCIABLE AT DUDLEY'S
DANCING THE "WEEVILY WHEAT."

"Good night, Lettie!"
"Goodnight, Ben!"
(The moon is sinking at the west.)
"Good night, my sweetheart." Once again
The parting kiss, while comrades wait
Impatient at the roadside gate,
And the red moon sinks beyond the west.

THE SOCIABLE AT DUDLEY'S.

I.

JOHN JENNINGS was not one of those men who go to a donation party with fifty cents' worth of potatoes and eat and carry away two dollars' worth of turkey and jelly-cake. When he drove his team around to the front door for Mrs. Jennings, he had a sack of flour and a quarter of a fine fat beef in his sleigh and a five-dollar bill in his pocket-book, a contribution to Elder Wheat's support.

Milton, his twenty-year-old son, was just driving out of the yard, seated in a fine new cutter, drawn by a magnificent gray four-year-old colt. He drew up as Mr. Jennings spoke.

"Now be sure and don't never leave him a minute untied. And see that the harness is all right. Do you hear, Milton?"

"Yes, I hear!" answered the young fellow, rather impatiently, for he thought himself old enough and big enough to look out for himself.

"Don't race, will y', Milton?" was his mother's anxious question from the depth of her shawls.

"Not if I can help it," was his equivocal response as he chirruped to Marc Antony. The grand brute made a rearing leap that brought a cry from the mother and a laugh from the young driver, and swung into the road at a flying pace. The night was clear and cold, the sleighing excellent, and the boy's heart was full of exultation.

It was a joy just to control such a horse as he drew rein over that night. Large, with the long, lithe body of a tiger and the broad, clear limbs of an elk, the gray colt strode away up the road, his hoofs flinging a shower of snow over the dasher. The lines were like steel rods; the sleigh literally swung by them; the traces hung slack inside the thills. The bells clashed out a swift clamor; the runners seemed to hiss over the snow as the duck-breasted cutter swung round the curves and softly rose and fell along the undulating road.

On either hand the snow stood billowed against the fences and amid the wide fields of corn-stalks bleached in the wind. Over in the east, above the line of timber skirting Cedar Creek, the vast, slightly gibbous moon was rising, sending along the crusted snow a broad path of light. Other sleighs could be heard through the still, cold air. Far away a party of four or five were singing a chorus as they spun along the road.

Something sweet and unnamable was stirring in the young fellow's brain as he spun along in the marvelously still and radiant night. He wished Eileen were with him. The vast and cloudless blue vault of sky glittered with stars, which even the radiant moon could not dim. Not a breath of air was stirring save that made by the swift, strong stride of the horse.

It was a night for youth and love and bells, and Milton felt this consciously, and felt it by singing:

"Stars of the summer night,
  Hide in your azure deeps,—
  She sleeps—my lady sleeps."

He was on his way to get Bettie Moss, one of his old sweethearts, who had become more deeply concerned with the life of Edwin Blackler. He had taken the matter with sunny philosophy even before meeting Eileen Deering at the Seminary, and he was now on his way to bring about peace between Ed and Bettie, who had lately quarreled. Incidentally he expected to enjoy the sleigh-ride.

"Stiddy, boy! Ho, boy! *Stiddy*, old fellow," he called soothingly to Marc, as he neared the gate and whirled up to the door. A girl came to the door as he drove up, her head wrapped in a white hood, a shawl on her arms. She had been waiting for him.

"Hello, Milt. That you?"

"It's me. Been waiting?"

"I should say I had. Begun t' think you'd gone back on me. Everybody else's gone."

"Well! Hop in here before you freeze; we'll not be the last ones there. Yes, bring the shawl; you'll need it t' keep the snow off your face," he called, authoritatively.

"'Tain't snowin', is it?" she asked as she shut the door and came to the sleigh's side.

"Clear as a bell," he said as he helped her in.

"Then where'll the snow come from?"

"From Marc's heels."

"Goodness sakes! you don't expect me t' ride after *that* wild-headed critter, do you?"

His answer was a chirp which sent Marc half-way to the gate before Bettie could catch her breath. The reins stiffened in his hands. Bettie clung to him, shrieking at every turn in the road.

"Milton Jennings, if you tip us over, I'll"——

Milton laughed, drew the colt down to a steady, swift stride, and Bettie put her hands back under the robe.

"I wonder who that is ahead?" he asked after a few minutes, which brought them in sound of bells.

"I guess it's Cy Hurd; it sounded like his bells when he went past. I guess it's him and Bill an' Belle an' Cad Hines."

"Expect to see Ed there?" asked Milton after a little pause.

"I don't care whether I ever see him again or not," she snapped.

"Oh, yes, you do!" he answered, feeling somehow her insincerity.

"Well—I don't!"

Milton didn't care to push the peace-making any further. However, he had curiosity enough to ask, "What upset things 'tween you 'n Ed?"

"Oh, nothing."

"You mean none o' my business?"

"I didn't say so."

"No, you didn't need to," he laughed, and she joined in.

"Yes, that's Cy Hurd. I know that laugh of his far's I c'n hear it," said Bettie as they jingled along. "I wonder who's with him?"

"We'll mighty soon see," said Milton, as he wound the lines around his hands and braced his feet, giving a low whistle, which seemed to run through the colt's blood like fire. His stride did not increase in rate, but its reach grew majestic as he seemed to lengthen and lower. His broad feet flung great disks of hard-packed snow over the dasher, and under the clash of his bells the noise of the other team grew plainer.

"Get out of the way," sang Milton, as he approached the other team. There was challenge and exultation in his tone.

"Hello! In a hurry?" shouted those in front, without increasing their own pace.

"Ya-as, something of a hurry," drawled Milton in a disguised voice.

"Wa-al? Turn out an' go by if you are."

"No, thankee, I'll just let m' nag nibble the hay out o' your box an' take it easy."

"Sure o' that?"

"You bet high I am." Milton nudged Bettie, who was laughing with delight. "It's Bill an' his bays. He thinks there isn't a team in the country can keep up with him. Get out o' the way there!" he shouted again. "I'm in a hurry."

"Let 'em out! Let 'em out, Bill," they heard Cy say, and the bays sprang forward along the level road, the bells ringing like mad, the snow flying, the girls screaming at every lurch of the sleighs. But Marc's head still shook haughtily above the end-gate; still the foam from his lips fell upon the hay in the box ahead.

"Git out o' this! Yip!" yelled Bill to his bays, but Marc merely made a lunging leap and tugged at the lines as if asking for more liberty. Milton gave him his head and laughed to see the great limbs rise and fall like the pistons of an engine. They swept over the weeds like a hawk skimming the stubble of a wheat field.

"Get out o' the way or I'll run right over your back," yelled Milton again.

"Try it," was the reply.

"Grab hold of me, Bettie, and lean to the right. When we turn this corner I'm going to take the inside track and pass 'em."

"You'll tip us over"——

"No, I won't! Do as I tell you."

They were nearing a wide corner, where the road turned to the right and bore due south through the woods. Milton caught sight of the turn, gave a quick twist of the lines around his hands, leaned over the dasher and spoke shrilly:

"Git out o' this, Marc!"

The splendid brute swerved to the right and made a leap that seemed to lift the sleigh and all into the air. The snow flew in such stinging showers Milton could see nothing. The sleigh was on one runner, heeling like a yacht in a gale; the girl was clinging to his neck; he could hear the bells of the other sleigh to his left; Marc was passing them; he heard shouts and the swish of a whip. Another convulsive effort of the gray, and then Milton found himself in the road again, in the moonlight, where the apparently unwearied horse, with head out-thrust, nostril wide-blown and body squared, was trotting like a veteran on the track. The team was behind.

"Stiddy, boy!"

Milton soothed Marc down to a long, easy pace; then turned to Bettie, who had uncovered her face again.

"How d' y' like it?"

"My sakes! I don't want any more of that. If I'd 'a' known you was goin' t' drive like that I wouldn't 'a' come. You're worse'n Ed. I expected every minute we'd be down in the ditch. But, oh! ain't he jest splendint?" she added, in admiration of the horse.

"Don't y' want to drive him?"

"Oh, yes; let me try. I drive our teams."

She took the lines, and at Milton's suggestion wound them around her hands. She looked very pretty with the moon shining on her face, her eyes big and black with excitement, and Milton immediately put his arm around her and laid his head on her shoulder.

"Milton Jennings, you don't"——

"Look out," he cried in mock alarm, "don't you drop those lines!" He gave her a severe hug.

"Milton Jennings, you let go me!"

"That's what you said before."

"Take these lines."

"Can't do it," he laughed; "my hands are cold. Got to warm them, see?" He pulled off his mitten and put his icy hand under her chin. The horse was going at a tremendous pace again.

"O-o-o-oh! If you don't take these lines I'll drop 'em, so there!"

"Don't y' do it," he called warningly, but she did, and boxed his ears soundly while he was getting Marc in hand again. Bettie's rage was fleeting as the blown breath from Marc's nostrils, and when Milton turned to her again all was as if his deportment had been grave and cavalier.

The stinging air made itself felt, and they drew close under their huge buffalo robes as Marc strode steadily forward. The dark groves fell behind, the clashing bells marked the rods and miles and kept time to the songs they hummed.

"Jingle, bells! Jingle, bells!
 Jingle all the way.
 Oh, what joy it is to ride
 In a one-horse open sleigh."

They overtook another laughing, singing load of young folks—a great wood sleigh packed full with boys and girls, two and two—hooded girls, and boys with caps drawn down over their ears. A babel of tongues arose from the sweeping, creaking bob-sleigh, and rose into the silent air like a mighty peal of laughter.

II.

A SCHOOL-HOUSE set beneath the shelter of great oaks was the center of motion and sound. On one side of it the teams stood shaking their bells under their insufficient blankets, making a soft chorus of fitful trills heard in the pauses of the merry shrieks of the boys playing "pom-pom pullaway" across the road before the house, which radiated light and laughter. A group of young men stood on the porch as Milton drove up.

"Hello, Milt," said a familiar voice as he reined Marc close to the step.

"That you, Shep?"

"Chuss, it's me," replied Shep.

"How'd you know me so far off?"

"Puh! Don't y' s'pose I know that horse an' those bells—Miss Moss, allow me"——He helped her out with elaborate courtesy. "The supper and the old folks are *here*, and the girls and boys and the fun is over to Dudley's," he explained as he helped Bettie out.

"I'll be back soon's I put my horse up," said Milton to Bettie. "You go in and get good 'n' warm, and then we'll go over to the house."

"I saved a place in the barn for you, Milt. I knew you'd never let Marc stand out in the snow," said Shephard as he sprang in beside Milton.

"I knew you would. What's the news? Is Ed here t'night?"

"Yeh-up. On deck with S'fye Kinney. It'll make him *swear* when he finds out who Bettie come with."

"Let him. Are the Yohe boys here?"

"Yep. They're alwiss on hand, like a sore thumb. Bill's been drinking, and is likely to give Ed trouble. He never'll give Bettie up without a fight. Look out he don't jump onto *your* neck."

"No danger o' that," said Milton coolly.

The Yohe boys were strangers in the neighborhood. They had come in with the wave of harvest help from the South and had stayed on into the winter, making few friends and a large number of enemies among the young men of "the crick." Everybody admitted that they had metal in them, for they instantly paid court to the prettiest girls in the neighborhood, without regard to any prior claims.

And the girls were attracted by these Missourians, their air of mysterious wickedness and their muscular swagger, precisely as a flock of barnyard fowl are interested in the strange bird thrust among them.

But the Southerners had muscles like wild-cats, and their feats of broil and battle commanded a certain respectful consideration. In fact, most of the young men of the district were afraid of the red-faced, bold-eyed strangers, one of the few exceptions being Milton, and another Shephard Watson, his friend and room-mate at the Rock River Seminary. Neither of these boys being at all athletic, it was rather curious that Bill and Joe Yohe should treat them with so much consideration.

Bill was standing before the huge cannon stove, talking with Bettie, when Milton and Shephard returned to the school-house. The man's hard, black eyes were filled with a baleful fire, and his wolfish teeth shone through his long red mustache. It made Milton mutter under his breath to see how innocently Bettie laughed with him. She never dreamed and could not have comprehended the vileness of the man's whole life and thought. No lizard reveled in the mud more hideously than he. His conversation reeked with obscenity. His tongue dropped poison each moment when among his own sex, and his eye blazed it forth when in the presence of women.

"Hello, Bill," said Milton, with easy indifference. "How goes it?"

"Oh, 'bout so-so. You rather got ahead o' me t'night, didn't yeh?"

"Well, rather. The man that gets ahead o' me has got t' drive a good team, eh?" He looked at Bettie.

"I'd like to try it," said Bill.

"Well, let's go across the road," said Milton to Bettie, anxious to get her out of the way of Bill.

They had to run the gauntlet of the whooping boys outside, but Bettie proved too fleet of foot for them all.

When they entered the Dudley house opposite, her cheeks were hot with color, but the roguish gleam in her eyes changed to a curiously haughty and disdainful look as she passed Blackler, who stood desolately beside the door, looking awkward and sullen.

Milton was a great favorite, and he had no time to say anything more to Bettie as peace-maker. He reached Ed as soon as possible.

"Ed, what's up between you and Bettie?"

"Oh, I don't know. I can't find out," Blackler replied, and he spurred himself desperately into the fun.

III.

"IT'LL make Ed Blackler squirm t' see Betsey come in on Milt Jennings' arm," said Bill to Shephard after Milton went out.

"Wal, chuss. I denk it will." Shephard was looking round the room, where the old people were noisily eating supper, and the steaming oysters and the cold chicken's savory smell went to his heart. One of the motherly managers of the feast bustled up to him.

"Shephard, you c'n run over t' the house an' tell the young folks that they can come over t' supper about eight o'clock; that'll be in a half an hour. You understand?"

"Oh, I'm so hungry! Can't y' give me a hunk o' chicken t' stay m' stomach?"

Mrs. Councill laughed. "I'll fish you out a drumstick," she said. And he went away, gnawing upon it hungrily. Bill went with him, still belching forth against Blackler.

"Jim said he heard *he* said he'd slap my face f'r a cent. I wish he would. I'd lick the life out of 'im in a minnit."

"Why don't you pitch into Milt? He's got her now. He's the one y'd orto be dammin'."

"Oh, he don't mean nothin' by it. He don't care for her. I saw him down to town at the show with the girl he's after. He's jest makin' Ed mad."

A game of "Copenhagen" was going on as they entered. Bettie was in the midst of it, but Milton, in the corner, was looking on and talking with a group of those who had outgrown such games.

The ring of noisy, flushed and laughter-intoxicated young people filled the room nearly to the wall, and round and round the ring flew Bettie, pursued by Joe Yohe.

"Go it, Joe!" yelled Bill.

"You're good f'r 'im," yelled Shephard.

Milton laughed and clapped his hands. "Hot foot, Bettie!"

Like another Atalanta, the superb young girl sped, now dodging through the ring, now doubling as her pursuer tried to catch her by turning back. At last she made the third circuit, and, breathless and laughing, took her place in the line. But Joe rushed upon her, determined to steal a kiss anyhow.

"H'yare! H'yare! None o' that."

"That's no fair," cried the rest, and he was caught by a dozen hands.

"She didn't go round three times," he said.

"Yes, she did," cried a dozen voices.

"You shut up," he retorted, brutally, looking at Ed Blackler, who had not spoken at all. Ed glared back, but said nothing. Bettie ignored Ed, and the game went on.

"There's going to be trouble here to-night," said Milton to Shephard.

Shephard, as the ring dissolved, stepped into the middle of the room and flourished his chicken-leg as if it were a baton. After the burst of laughter, his sonorous voice made itself heard.

"Come to supper! Everybody take his girl if he can, and if he can't—get the other feller's girl."

Bill Yohe sprang toward Bettie, but Milton had touched her on the arm.

"Not t'night, Bill," he grinned.

Bill grinned in reply and made off toward another well-known belle, Ella Pratt, who accepted his escort. Ed Blackler, with gloomy desperation, took Maud Buttles, the most depressingly plain girl in the room, an action that did not escape Bettie's eyes, and which softened her heart toward him; but she did not let him see it.

Supper was served on the desks, each couple seated in the drab-colored wooden seats as if they were at school. A very comfortable arrangement for those who occupied the back seats, but torture to the adults who were obliged to cramp their legs inside the desk where the primer class sat on school-days.

Bettie saw with tenderness how devotedly poor Ed served Maud. He could not have taken a better method of heaping coals of fire on her head.

Ed was entirely unconscious of her softening, however, for he could not look around from where he sat. He heard her laughing and believed she was happy. He had not taken poor Maud for the purpose of showing his penitence, for he had no such feeling in his heart; he was, on the contrary, rather gloomy and reckless. He was not in a mood to show a front of indifference.

The oysters steamed; the heels of the boys' boots thumped in wild delight; the women bustled about; the girls giggled, and the men roared with laughter. Everybody ate as if he and she had never tasted oyster-soup and chicken before, and the cakes and pies went the way of the oyster-soup like corn before a troup of winter turkeys.

Bill Yohe, by way of a joke, put some frosting down the back of Cy Hurd, and, by way of delicate attention to Ella, alternately shoved her out of the seat and pulled her back again, while Joe hurled a chicken-leg at Cad Hines as she stood in the entry-way. Will Kinney told Sary Hines for the fourth time how his team had run away, interrupted by his fear that some kind of pie would get away untasted.

"An' so I laid the lines down—H'yare! Gimme another handful of crackers, Merry—an' I laid the lines down while I went t' fine—nary a noyster I can hold any more. Mrs. Moss, I'm ready f'r pie now—an' so I noticed ole Frank's eye kind o' roll, but thinksi, I c'n git holt o' the lines if he—Yes'm, I alwiss eat mince; won't you try some, Sary?—an'—an'—so, jest as I gut my ax—You bet! I'm goin' t' try a piece of every kind if it busts my stummick. Gutta git my money's worth."

Milton was in his best mood and was very attractive in his mirth. His fine teeth shone and his yellow curls shook under the stress of his laughter. He wrestled with Bettie for the choice bits of cake, delighting in the touch of her firm, sweet flesh; and, as for Bettie, she was almost charmed to oblivion of Ed by the superior attractions of Milton's town-bred gallantry. Ed looked singularly awkward and lonesome as he sat sprawled out in one of the low seats, and curiously enough his uncouthness and disconsolateness of attitude won her heart back again.

Everybody, with the usual rustic freedom, had remarks to make upon the situation.

"Wal, Bettie, made a swop, hev yeh?" said Councill.

"Hello, Milt; thought you had a girl down town."

"Oh, I keep one at each end of the line," Milton replied, with his ready laugh.

"Wal, I swan t' gudgeon! I can't keep track o' you town fellers. You're too many f'r me!" said Mrs. Councill.

Carrie Hines came up behind Milton and Bettie and put her arms around their necks, bringing their cheeks together. Bettie grew purple with anger and embarrassment, but Milton, with his usual readiness, said, "Thank you," and reached for the tittering malefactor's waist. Nobody noticed it, for the room was full of such romping.

The men were standing around the stove discussing political outlooks, and the matrons were busy with the serving of the supper. Out of doors the indefatigable boys were beginning again on "pom-pom pullaway."

Supper over, the young folks all returned to the house across the way, leaving the men of elderly blood to talk on the Grange and the uselessness of the middlemen. Sport began again in the Dudley farm-house by a dozen or so of the young people "forming on" for "Weevily Wheat."

"Weevily Wheat" was a "donation dance." As it would have been wicked to have a fiddle to play the music, singers were substituted with stirring effect, and a song was sung, while the couples bowed and balanced and swung in rhythm to it:

"Come *hither*, my love, and *trip* together
In the morning early.
I'll give to *you* the parting hand,
Although I love you dearly.
But I *won't* have none of y'r weevily wheat,
An' I *won't* have *none* of y'r barley,
But have some flour in a half an hour
To bake a cake for Charley.

"Oh, Charley, *he* is a fine young man;
Charley, he is a dandy.
Oh, Charley, *he's* a fine young man,
F'r he buys the girls some candy.
Oh, I *won't* have none o' y'r weevily wheat,
I won't have *none* o' y'r barley,
But have some flour in a half an hour
To bake a cake for Charley.

"Oh, Charley, he's," etc.

Milton was soon in the thick of this most charming old-fashioned dance, which probably dates back to dances on the green in England or Norway. Bettie was a good dancer, and as she grew excited with the rhythm and swing of the quaint, plaintive music her form grew supple at the waist and her large limbs light. The pair moved up and back between the two ranks of singers, then down the outside, and laughed in glee when they accelerated the pace at the time when they were swinging down the center. All faces were aglow and eyes shining.

Bill's red face and bullet eyes were not beautiful, but the grace and power of his body were unmistakable. He was excited by the music, the alcohol he had been drinking, and by the presence of the girls, and threw himself into the play with dangerous abandon.

Under his ill-fitting coat his muscles rolled swift and silent. His tall boots were brilliantly blue and starred with gold at the top, and his pantaloons were tucked inside the tops to let their glory strike the eye. His physical strength and grace and variety of "steps" called forth many smiles and admiring exclamations from the girls, and caused the young men to lose interest in "Weevily Wheat."

When a new set was called for, Bill made a determined assault on Bettie and secured her, for she did not have the firmness to refuse. But the singers grew weary, and the set soon broke up. A game of forfeit was substituted. This also dwindled down to a mere excuse for lovers to kiss each other, and the whole company soon separated into little groups to chatter and romp. Some few sat at the table in the parlor and played "authors."

Bettie was becoming annoyed by the attentions of Bill, and, to get rid of him, went with Miss Lytle, Milton and two or three others into another room and shut the door. This was not very unusual, but poor Blackler seemed to feel it a direct affront to him and was embittered. He was sitting by Ella Pratt when Bill Yohe swaggered up to him.

"Say! Do you know where your girl is?"

"No, an' I don't care."

"Wal! It's *time* y' cared. She's in the other room there. Milt Jennings has cut you out."

"You're a liar," cried the loyal lover, leaping to his feet.

Spat! Yohe's open palm resounded upon the pale face of Blackler, whose eyes had a wild glare in them, and the next moment they were rolling on the floor like a couple of dogs, the stronger and older man above, the valiant lover below. The house resounded with sudden screams, and then came the hurry of feet, then a hush, in the midst of which was heard the unsubdued voice of Blackler as he rose to his feet.

"You're a"——

Another dull stroke with the knotted fist, and the young fellow went to the floor again, while Joe Yohe, like a wild beast roused at the sight of blood, stood above the form of his brother (who had leaped upon the fallen man), shouting with the hoarse, raucous note of a tiger:

"Give 'im hell! I'll back yeh."

Bettie pushed through the ring of men and women who were looking on in delicious horror—pushed through quickly and yet with dignity. Her head was thrown back, and the strange look on her face was thrilling. Facing the angry men with a gesture of superb scorn and fearlessness, she spoke, and in the deep hush her quiet words were strangely impressive:

"Bill Yohe, what do you think you're doing?"

For a moment the men were abashed, and, starting back, they allowed Blackler, dazed, bleeding and half strangled, to rise to his feet. He would have sprung against them both, for he had not heard or realized who was speaking, but Bettie laid her hand on his arm, and the haughty droop of her eyelids changed as she said in a tender voice:

"Never mind, Ed; they ain't worth mindin'!"

Her usual self came back quickly as she led him away. Friends began to mutter now, and the swagger of the brothers threatened further trouble. Their eyes rolled, their knotted hands swung about like bludgeons. Threats, horrible snarls and oaths poured from their lips. But there were heard at this critical moment rapid footsteps—a round, jovial voice—and bursting through the door came the great form and golden head of Lime Gilman.

"Hold on here! What's all this?" he said, leaping with an ominously good-natured smile into the open space before the two men, whose restless pacing stopped at the sound of his voice. His sunny, laughing blue eyes swept around him, taking in the situation at a glance. He continued to smile, but his teeth came together.

"Git out o' this, you hounds! Git!" he said, in the same jovial tone. "You! *You*," he said to Bill, slapping him lightly on the breast with the back of his lax fingers. Bill struck at him ferociously, but the slope-shouldered giant sent it by with his left wrist, kicking the feet of the striker from under him with a frightful swing of his right foot—a trick which appalled Joe.

"Clear the track there," ordered Lime. "It's against the law t' fight at a donation; so out y' go."

Bill crawled painfully to his feet.

"I'll pay you for this yet."

"*Any* time but now. Git out, 'r I'll kick you out." Lime's voice changed now. The silent crowd made way for them, and, seizing Joe by the shoulder and pushing Bill before him, the giant passed out into the open air. There he pushed Bill off the porch into the snow, and kicked his brother over him with this parting word:

"You infernal hyenies! Kickin's too good f'r you. If you ever want me, look around an' you'll find me."

Then, to the spectators who thronged after, he apologized:

"I hate t' fight, and especially to kick a man; but they's times when a man's *got* t' do it. Now, jest go back and have a good time. Don't let them hyenies spoil all y'r fun."

That ended it. All knew Lime. Everybody had heard how he could lift one end of the separator and toss a two-bushel sack filled with wheat over the hind wheel of a wagon, and the terror of his kick was not unknown to them. They all felt sure that the Yohes would not return, and all went back into the house and attempted to go on with the games. But it was impossible; such exciting events must be discussed, and the story was told and retold by each one.

When Milton returned to the parlor, he saw Bettie, tender, dignified and grave, bending over Blackler, bathing his bruised face. Milton had never admired her more than at that moment; she looked so womanly. She no longer cared what people thought.

The other girls, pale and tearful and a little hysterical, stood about, close to their sweethearts. They enjoyed the excitement, however, and the fight appealed to something organic in them.

The donation party was at an end, that was clear, and the people began to get ready to go home. Bettie started to thank Lyman for his help.

"Don't say anything. I'd 'a' done it jest the same f'r anybody. It ain't the thing to come to a donation and git up a row."

Milton hardly knew whether to ask Bettie to go back with him or not, but Blackler relieved him from embarrassment by rousing up and saying:

"Oh, I'm all right now, Bettie. Hyere's yer girl, Milt. See the eye I've got on me? She says she won't ride home with any such"——

"Ed, what in the world do you mean?" Bettie could hardly understand her lover's sudden exultation; it was still a very serious matter to her, in spite of the complete reconciliation which had come with the assault. She felt in a degree guilty, and that feeling kept her still tearful and subdued, but Ed leered and winked with his good eye in uncontrollable delight. Milton turned to Bettie at last, and said:

"Well! I'll get Marc around to the door in a few minutes. Get your things on."

Bettie and Ed stood close together by the door. She was saying:

"You'll forgive me, won't you, Ed?"

"Why, course I will, Bettie. I was as much to blame as you was. I no business to git mad till I knew what I was gittin' mad *at.*"

They were very tender now.

"I'll—I'll go home with you, if you want me to, 'stead of with Milt," she quavered.

"No, I've got to take S'fye home. It's the square thing."

"All right, Ed, but come an' let me talk it all straight."

"It's all straight now; let's let it all go, whaddy y' say?"

"All right, Ed."

There was a kiss that the rest pretended not to hear. And bidding them all good-night, Bettie ran out to the fence, where Milton sat waiting.

The moon was riding high in the clear, cold sky, but falling toward the west, as they swung into the wood-road. Through the branches of the oaks the stars, set in the deep-blue, fathomless night, peered cold and bright. There was no wind save the rush of air caused by the motion of the sleigh. Neither of the young people spoke for some time. They lay back in the sleigh under the thick robes, listening to the chime of the bells, the squeal of the runners, and the weirdly-sweet distant singing of another sleigh-load of young people far ahead.

Milton pulled Marc down to a slow trot, and, tightening his arm around Bettie's shoulders in a very brotherly hug, said:

"Well, I'm glad you and Ed have fixed things up again. You'd always have been sorry."

"It was all my fault anyway," replied the girl, with a little tremor in her voice, "and it was all my fault to-night, too. I no business to 'a' gone off an' left him that way."

"Well, it's all over now anyway, and so I wouldn't worry any more about it," said Milton, soothingly, and then they fell into silence again.

The sagacious Marc Antony strode steadily away, and the two young lovers went on with their dreaming. Bettie was silent mainly, and Milton was trying to fancy that she was Eileen, and was remembering the long rides they had had together. And the horse's hoofs beat a steady rhythm, the moon fell to the west, and the bells kept cheery chime. The breath of the horse rose into the air like steam. The house-dogs sent forth warning howls as they went by. Once or twice they passed houses where the windows were still lighted and where lanterns were flashing around the barn, where the horses were being put in for the night.

The lights were out at the home of Bettie when they drove up, for the young people, however rapidly they might go to the sociable, always returned much slower than the old folks. Milton leaped out and held up his arms to help his companion out. As she shook the robes down, stood up and reached out for his arms, he seized her round the waist, and, holding her clear of the ground, kissed her in spite of her struggles.

"Milton!"

"The las' time, Bettie; the las' time," he said, in extenuation. With this mournful word on his lips he leaped into the sleigh and was off like the wind. But the listening girl heard his merry voice ringing out on the still air. Suddenly something sweet and majestic swept upon the girl. Something that made her look up into the glittering sky with vast yearning. In the awful hush of the sky and the plain she heard the beat of her own blood in her ears. She longed for song to express the swelling of her throat and the wistful ache of her heart.

AN AFTERWORD:
OF WINDS, SNOWS AND THE STARS

O witchery of the winter night
(With broad moon shouldering to the west)!

In city streets the west wind sweeps
Before my feet in rustling flight;
The midnight snows in untracked heaps
Lie cold and desolate and white.
I stand and wait with upturned eyes,
Awed with the splendor of the skies
And star-trained progress of the moon.

The city walls dissolve like smoke
Beneath the magic of the moon,
And age falls from me like a cloak;
I hear sweet girlish voices ring
Clear as some softly stricken string—
(The moon is sailing to the west.)
The sleigh-bells clash in homeward flight;
With frost each horse's breast is white—
(The big moon sinking to the west.)

"Good night, Lettie!"
"Good night, Ben!"
(The moon is sinking at the west.)
"Good night, my sweetheart," Once again
The parting kiss while comrades wait
Impatient at the roadside gate,
And the red moon sinks beyond the west.
